The Short Stories of Letitia Elizabeth Landon

Volume II

Letitia Elizabeth Landon was born on the 14th August 1802 in Chelsea, London.

A precocious child she had her first poem published is 1820 using the single 'L' as her marker. The following year her first volume appeared and sold well. She published a further two poems that same year with just the initials 'L.E.L." It provided the basis for much intrigue.

She becáme the chief reviewer of the Gazette and published her second collection, 'The Improvisatrice', in 1824.

By 1826, rumours began to circulate that she had had affairs. For several years they continued to circulate until she broke off an engagement when her betrothed, upon further investigation, found them to be unfounded. Her words reflect the lack of trust she felt "The mere suspicion is dreadful as death"

On June 7th 1838 she married George Maclean, initially in secret, and a month later they sailed to the Cape Coast.

However, the marriage proved to be short lived as on October 15th, that same year, Letitia was found dead, a bottle of prussic acid in her hand.

Index of Contents

REBECCA

How beautiful, buoyant, and glad is morning! The first sunshine on the leaves; the first wind, laden with the first breath of the flowers—that deep sigh with which they seem to waken from sleep; the first dew, untouched even by the light foot of the early hare; the first chirping of the rousing birds, as if eager to begin song and flight: all is redolent of the strength given by rest, and the joy of conscious life.

Rebecca Clinton, though pale with the long vigil of an anxious night—such as is spent by a sick bedside—felt the revigorating influence. She opened the lattice of her little chamber, and it shook from the rose-tree, with which it was overgrown, a shower of dew-drops and leaves. So close that it must have been hidden amid the foliage of a huge old horse-chestnut tree, though not a leaf stirred, a cuckoo was singing—the only bird whose chant was yet complete. Rebecca leant listening to the soft but mournful reiteration, with the tears fast rushing into her eyes. Sound peculiarly appeals to memory. On awakening from her brief but heavy slumber, she had almost unconsciously thrown open the window; the fresh air, the clear atmosphere, gave for a moment their own joyfulness to her spirits: but that song broke the spell. She turned away, and, with the common exaggeration of much sorrow, reproached the bright and unsympathising morning; while the two sad and still-repeated notes seemed the very echo of her thoughts.

At length she rose, and with a light step sought the adjacent apartment. Hung with old, worm-eaten tapestry, and massy curtains that excluded the light, a floor dark from age, and the ancient chairs and bureau formed of the black walnut-tree wood,—it seemed indeed the chamber of death. Rebecca could scarcely penetrate the obscurity; gradually her sight became accustomed to the darkness, and surrounding objects stood forth dimly visible. "I have slept more than an hour," thought she, as her eye fell upon the glass, whose sands had run out; and it comforted her to observe that the cup of herb-tea was untouched.

Noiselessly she drew near the bed, and, with careful hand removing one of the thick folds of the curtains, was able to gaze on the visage of the sleeper, which was turned directly towards her. She started, as if the face had not been a familiar one; but now, that no expression illumined the countenance, no affection spoke in the closed eyes—now she could see the ravages of disease. Every feature was sharp, the forehead was sunken, and the cheek was so white that it was undistinguishable from the pillow on which it lay. Even in sleep the cold damp stood on the brow, and the breath was drawn with an effort. She let the curtain fall, but softly; and left the room for her own. There she gave way; and the wrung hand, the deep sob, betrayed without relieving the passion of grief.

Rebecca was an only and an orphan child, and her father had idolised her with a twofold fondness. He loved in her both her mother and herself; and the love was the deeper, because that on it rested the tenderness of the grave. Each felt they had the place of another to supply.

Clinton was of an old but decayed family; he had lost the wreck of his property by fighting for the Stuarts, and the Restoration brought only those unfulfilled hopes which seem sent but to make disappointment more bitter. To an aged servant, who had lived beneath his roof in better days, he owed his present asylum; she had been left housekeeper at the manor while its proprietor was abroad, and three rooms were made serviceable to her old master and his daughter. Rebecca was now about twenty; and from her mother, a converted Jewess, she inherited that Oriental style of beauty which enables us to comprehend the similes of the Eastern poets. Truly had she the dark full eye of the gazelle, the grace of the young cedar, and a blush coloured from the earliest rose in Sharon. She was impetuous and imaginative; the impetuosity had been little called forth by the solitude in which they lived, but the imagination had been strongly nourished. Their small shelf held a few volumes—some early romances and works of the later dramatists gave their own poetry to the ideal world which filled all her lonely hours. Her affection for her father was entire and engrossing: it must be owned, that its unity had never been endangered; for, from the verge of girlhood, their seclusion had been unbroken save by a single visitor; and he was little calculated to attract a romantic and youthful female.

Richard Vernon was one of those religious enthusiasts with which the period abounded. Naturally stern and harsh in temper as in feature, he delighted in sacrifice: from it he drew an inward consolation of superiority, and rejoiced in the scorn he cast on the pleasures and pursuits of other men. His mind was strong, but narrow; and his enthusiasm had never known but one vent. Embittered by the consciousness of unappreciated talent, spiritual pride had become a tower of refuge: believing himself to be the chosen of the Lord, accounted for and sanctified the neglect of men: was not the curse of blindness on all but the elect?—"Seeing ye shall see, and shall not perceive; and hearing ye shall hear, and shall not understand."

Of an iron constitution, he had never known those bodily weaknesses which so often affect the feelings; and nothing teaches like sickness the value of patience and sympathy. He had been left an orphan at an early age—too early for memory—and had forced his own hard way in a hard world: love had never made the excitement of his youth, nor the relaxation of his manhood. In short, he had passed through life without having experienced one softening influence. From sickness he never learnt the worth of kindness, nor had death ever taught him how sacred and how bitter is the thought of the beloved and of the dead. He had belonged to the church, from which, however, he had been ejected for non-conformity.

The loss of his benefice was small to him, in comparison with many of his brethren; for death succeeding death had put him in possession of much property belonging to distant relatives. Not such was the indignation with which he beheld the obedience exacted, and the authority exercised by the episcopal church. The dark and mysterious passages of Scripture became more than ever his constant study; and applying every denunciation to his own time, he firmly believed that judgment was at hand, and only waited some crowning iniquity to call down God's vengeance on a guilty land.

It is a humbling thing to human pride to observe that strength of mind does not preserve its possessor from indulging any favourite delusion; but that this very strength gives its own force to the belief. In the eyes of Richard Vernon all the pleasures and employments of his fellow-men were abomination and vanity; business was a heaping up of worthless dross; intellect, a stumbling-block; poetry, painting, and music, devices of the enemy; affection, sinful weakness: indeed, all worldly pursuits were foolishness, if not sin, in those who were now warned to "flee from the wrath to come." Still, even while he deemed himself most secure, the softest yet most powerful of earthly feelings had taken a firm hold of his heart.

No two men could be of more opposite dispositions and habits than Vernon and Clinton; the latter had delicate health and a gentle temper—was at once humble and rational in his piety—and had all the elegant and refined tastes which the other despised. Still, since their residence in the same neighbourhood, their intercourse had been constant. Clinton was fond of society, though now compelled by circumstances to renounce it. The very fact of having to support his opinions was an excitement; and the often fiery eloquence of the fierce Calvinist had for him all the enjoyment of poetry. Vernon liked the meek and kind-hearted invalid more than he would himself have admitted; but the link that bound them together was the innocent and lovely Rebecca.

In the high, haughty temper of the young and queen-like beauty, Vernon recognised a similar spirit to his own, but which he was too conscious of his powers to fear, as a weaker-minded man might have done. One lesson from early experience—one touch of more delicate feeling—and Rebecca's heart might have been his. Though his age doubled hers, and his personal appearance was harsh even to forbiddingness, she might have loved him.

It is the mistake of a coxcomb, whose experience of affection is all to come—if it ever comes—to say that women are won by mere good looks. Though it does not owe its birth to them. Gratitude and Vanity are the nurses that rock the cradle of Love. Neither of these did Vernon deign to conciliate. Angry at a feeling with which he nevertheless struggled in vain, the conflict gave even additional harshness to his manner; and he contradicted Rebecca's opinions, reproached her likings, disdained her pursuits, and dealt out condemnation on all her favourite volumes, as if not allowing his external demeanour to be affected were some excuse for his internal preference.

About a month before the period of which we are now speaking, he had openly offered himself as suitor to Rebecca Clinton. One evening, when his temper had been softened by the patient suffering of her father—from which the conversation had taken an unusually subdued tone—the invalid was led, from alluding to his illness, to touch upon its consequences; and for a few minutes the image of his orphan girl destroyed all the firmness of his philosophy, all the resignation of religion. He was startled by Richard Vernon rising, and, with words vehement to fierceness, demanding his daughter Rebecca to wife.

Clinton was taken completely by surprise. Like most of those who daily see a child growing up before them, he had not calculated her years, and had never yet thought of Rebecca as of a woman. Though often, in some vague futurity, he had indulged in romance about her fortunes, better justified by her grace and loveliness than by the circumstances under which they were expanding; yet, certainly, the future he had imagined for her was not as the bride of Richard Vernon.

To balance these dreams there arose, on the instant, the many advantages of the proposal—her forlorn and desolate situation—and the high character of the man who now offered heart and home. Clinton gasped for breath, and gave a thankful consent.

At this moment Rebecca entered; but, alas! the proposal received a surprised, almost disdainful, refusal. As yet she knew too little of the worth of worldly advantages to estimate his disinterestedness at its value. Vernon left the house indignant and disappointed, but with less of anger and more of hope than Rebecca suspected. The truth is, he pitied her as a silly child, whose head was filled with old romances, and laid all the blame on her father's weak indulgence—an error he purposed to remedy with all convenient speed.

A sudden access of illness in Mr. Clinton made an excuse for calling, after a brief interval had elapsed; and his visits soon fell again into their usual train. Vernon was obstinate; and the refusal—which would have decided the refined, or discouraged the timid—was to him merely an obstacle to be subdued. Looking upon women as infinitely inferior to men, he was provoked to think that the whim of a foolish girl should interfere with his settled purpose. His first plan, that of calling in paternal authority to his assistance, was disappointed by Clinton's instant and decided declaration, that, even if he had the will, he did not consider he had the right to force the inclination of his daughter: his approbation and his preference were all he could give.

Vernon was more angry and discontented than disheartened, and more stubborn in his pursuit than ever, though he left its issue to circumstances, and perhaps his rebukes took even a severer tone. He deceived his own mind, and soothed his own pride, by the belief that he was only actuated by a desire for her temporal and spiritual benefit;—he knew he could save her from poverty; he equally presumed he could from perdition. A lamb rescued from the slaughter, a brand snatched from the fire, was the constant phraseology of his very thoughts.

Weakened by illness, worn by vague anxiety—the worst form anxiety can take—looking at all life's hopes and wishes through the shadows flung by coming death, Clinton dwelt upon his friend's offer till his strong wish grew, as wishes usually do, into a conviction that Rebecca would finally add her consent to his own.

Such was the state of the dwellers at the old house at the time when our tale commences.

Clinton, the morning his daughter bent over his feverish slumber, slept longer than usual, and was proportionably refreshed; and when Rebecca tempted him, in the afternoon, to the rustic seat beneath the sycamore—the pleasant shade around them, the bright sunshine elsewhere, the hum of the bees in the honied branches over-head, the chirping of the numerous birds, the gay colours of the flowers, almost unconsciously exerted a cheering influence; and their thoughts, though not glad, were at least placid and soothing. The lawn,—if lawn it could still be called, which had long lost the pristine smoothness of the once velvet turf, and was now covered with a multitude of daisies—signs, they say, of a poor soil, though it is, at all events, a cheerful poverty,—commanded a view of the adjacent country; and the road, varied by many a gentle undulation, wound through the hedge-girdled fields, some green with grass, others shining with the first yellow of the corn, and here and there an unenclosed nook where grew two or three stately elms.

Suddenly Rebecca's quick eye caught sight of a dark figure on one of the heights in the distance.

"How vexatious!" was her hasty exclamation; "here is Mr. Vernon coming to interrupt us!"

"I would, my child," replied Clinton mournfully, "you did more justice to the good qualities of a man who has the merit of appreciating yours. Rebecca! the time may, nay must come, when your only earthly resource will be the attachment of Richard Vernon. Do not interrupt me, dearest; if I pain you, it is for your good: but can you believe that your future desolate situation is ever absent from my mind? So young, so beautiful, and so unprotected—Rebecca, I could die in peace if you were the wife of Richard Vernon."

Rebecca rose from her seat on the grass, and, kneeling at her father's side, gazed for a few moments earnestly in his face before she replied.

"And would it content you, my father, to know that you had joined those whom nature hath sundered, O how utterly!—to know that your child was grown old even in her youth?—that she had thoughts she might not utter, hopes she herself must destroy?—that her daily words must be either mean with hypocrisy, or bitter with contention? A home! Is that a home by whose hearth sits coldness, and beneath whose roof is discontent? My father, I cannot love Richard Vernon! and that not for vain dislike to outward look or bearing, but because we have not one opinion, wish, or feeling in common. Even my weak judgment sees the fallacy of that morality which makes sins of innocent pleasures and of harmless employment; which renders the path of duty too rough and too narrow for human foot; and which wastes on vain trifles the salutary horror we intuitively feel of vice. I shudder at his religion. In the fierce damnation in which he delights, in the mystic revealments in which he exults, what trace is there of the meek and humble faith you have taught me should be my daily guide, extending its charity to all men? My father! you know that at your word I would wed Richard Vernon; but can you say that word?"

The only answer was a slight caress—it was enough; and Rebecca turned to re-enter the house. Glancing at the winding road, she saw that Vernon had yet a considerable space to cross before he could join them, and added cheerfully, "Fear not for me, my father; other fear"—and the rich colour mounted even to her crimsoned forehead—"other fear than that of want and privation befalling me, you cannot have. But I am strong in youth and in hope; I am skilful in many things; and it were strange, as well as hard, if I could not gain for myself the little I require."

What a visionary thing is the independence of youth! how full of projects, which take the shape of certainties! How much of rugged and stern experience it requires to convince the young and the eager, that the efforts of an individual unaided by connexion or circumstance, are the true reading of the allegory of the Danaides:—industry and skill, alas, how often are they but water drawn with labour into a bucket full of holes!

Clinton sat lost in thought, till he was roused by Vernon, who wore a gloomier brow, and spoke in even severer tones than usual.

"So, I find you alone! To be sure," said he, looking round, "you can see from hence the approach of any one, and any one can see your movements too."

Clinton replied but by asking his companion to sit down on the bench beside him; and in so doing, he displaced a small volume, whose worn black calf binding shewed it was a favourite. It fell open at the very play he and Rebecca had been reading, "The Merchant of Venice;" and the unfortunate book immediately suggested a new vent to Vernon's spleen.

"And this, forsooth, is the study of your noon! I marvel not that your daughter's head is so turned by vanities and fancies. Verily, poetry is a device of the evil one, which has served him in good sort!"

"A somewhat harsh judgment," returned Clinton, smiling, "to be pronounced on those who beguile many a weary hour, and to whom we owe many a delicate enjoyment."

"Now, out upon such toys! Were my power equal to my will, I would soon purify the land, even with fire, of each vain and lying tome that but distracts the mind from the one sacred volume, on which alone it should be fixed, and on which alone thought should meditate."

"Your pardon, friend," replied Clinton; "I do not believe that the heart is turned from the Creator by enjoying his works. Of what avail is the sweet breath of the rose, the morning song of the lark? The pleasure they impart is not matter of necessity, and yet we delight in both. The soul of the poet is as much His gift as the fragrance of the flower, or the lay of the bird; and the page where inspired words record heroic deed, touching sorrow, or natural loveliness, is one of those pleasures for which we should be thankful. I, for my part, believe most devoutly in the Almighty mercy, when I see how much that is beautiful and gladdening has been scattered over our pilgrimage here."

Vernon's attention had been diverted by a shadow flung on one of the windows. He watched, and could see that it was Rebecca; she was seated at work, with her back to the garden, which she seemed to have no design of visiting.

"I appear to have frightened away your daughter," exclaimed he, angrily.

"Most of our household occupations devolve on Rebecca," was her father's reply.

"I see how it is, and I weary of this childishness," retorted Vernon. "Reginald Clinton, for the last time I offer you the name and home of an honest man for your daughter. Perhaps, after the fashion of those vain romances in which you indulge, you deem that Rebecca has but to go forth, like some wandering princess, to find earl and knight ready to lay lance in rest 'pour l'amour de ses beaux yeux;' and that the coronet and the castle wait for their mistress. I warn you, this is not the reading of real life! Rebecca will enter the cold and cruel world, homeless, friendless, moneyless! Her refined nature will soon revolt at the meanness more than at the privation of poverty. Then will her beauty—for she is fair, very fair—catch the eye of some young cavalier (troth, and but our king trains them in goodly practices!): first there will be refusal and reserve; then pity and relief, and the woman's heart will be caught by some woman's toy; folly will succeed to fancy; and a few soft words will disperse in air all that her father and her Bible have taught.

"Nay, let me finish the picture," he continued, upon a somewhat impatient gesture of his friend. "After vanity comes disappointment—the lover tires, or she herself may change; the same tale is told by another, and the same sequel ensues—save that the love is not so deep, and the faith not so true. A few years, and her face is not fair as it was in youth—sin and sorrow have left on it their traces; the cheek has a bloom not its own, the hair is dashed with grey, the lip is thin, and the brow haggard. The lover turns away; and death comes on, heralded by poverty and neglect; then the child of your heart goes down to the grave unwept, her memory cursed by many whom she led to evil, to disobedience, and to waste. And what think you becomes of the immortal soul, base, polluted, and hardened in its guilt? Deem you that the gates of death will not be to such a one the gates of hell?" "I thank you for your kindly prophecy," said a low but firm voice beside him.

Rebecca, having caught the raised tones of Vernon, and fearing lest aught of discussion might weary her enfeebled father, had hurried to the spot; thus becoming the auditor of what was not meant for her hearing. She stood, the colour deepened into scarlet on her cheek, her lip curved with scorn, and, her dark eyebrows almost meeting in their indignation, while her large eyes flashed as if the pupil were indeed an orb turned by the soul to light, she continued: "I thank you; but now listen to my words, even as I have done to yours. Rather would I bear the doom your kindness has poured into the ear of a dying father, than be your wife!"

She said no more, but walked hastily away; and in another moment Vernon was seen hurrying along the winding road.

Clinton retired to rest sooner than usual; and his daughter took her accustomed seat, to watch during the earlier part of the night. He had slept, or seemed to sleep, for more than two hours, when suddenly he rose in his bed.

"Give me to drink, my child," he murmured almost inaudibly, yet with seeming effort.

She took the cup, and raised it to his mouth: but scarcely could her trembling hand replace it on the table, for she started to see the alteration in her father's face. "Open the window, love—the air is stifling."

Rebecca felt cold with the chill midnight, but she opened the heavy curtains and the casement, when a flood of dazzling moonlight poured into the dim room, and put the faint lamp to shame. A large branch of a chestnut-tree waved to and fro, whose leaves seemed filled with music; a sweet breeze came from the garden below, but sweet as it was, Clinton inspired it with difficulty. By a strong effort he put his hand beneath the pillow, and drew thence a small black book with silver clasps.

"Take it, my child; till this hour it has been my constant companion. Rebecca, it is your mother's Bible!"

Even as he spoke, his head sank on his daughter's shoulder; she moved not till the cheek pressed to hers grew like ice. One fearful shriek, and the living sank insensible by the side of the dead. A week afterwards, a funeral train was seen slowly winding through the wreathing honey-suckle and drooping ash which formed the green and glad road. There were only the coffin-bearers and two mourners—an aged woman and a young one, the housekeeper and Rebecca were following Reginald Clinton to his last resting-place; and ever and anon, as the coffin passed and brushed the boughs, heavy with their luxuriant foliage, a shower of fragrant leaves fell,—as if Summer wept over the sorrowful procession. Rebecca uncovered not her face till they reached the newly dug grave; she then cast one shuddering look, and again closed her veil. The service commenced, and a slight start spoke other emotion than grief, when she heard the voice of Richard Vernon begin the solemn ritual. It ended, and Rebecca remained motionless on her knee till her attention was awakened by that fearful and peculiar sound—a sound to which earth has no parallel—the rattle of the falling gravel on the coffin. She sprang forward. "Let me—let me gaze on him once again!"

She saw nothing but the black, damp mould, and sank back, unresisting, on the arm of Richard Vernon.

"My house is close at hand," said he, inquiringly to her aged companion.

"For the love of God, take her thither!" was the reply. "There is neither water nor aught else here; and she looks like one of the stone figures on the graves around us."

Rebecca was carried, still insensible, into the little parlour; and, with a tenderness that seemed foreign to his nature, Vernon placed her in a large antique settle, which he drew towards the window, fetched water, and left her and the good woman alone. Even when Rebecca revived, it was only for a while, to give way to bursts of passionate weeping. Old Hannah's affectionate soothing having at length calmed her, on rising to depart, she said to the bewildered girl, "We must thank Mr. Vernon before we go."

"This Mr. Vernon's house?" exclaimed Rebecca, turning yet paler.

"It is my house; and where could you be more welcome?" said its master.

Rebecca rose and thanked him for his kindness; and, touched by his obvious sympathy, as well as reassured by his reserved and unusually gentle manner, she did not refuse his request, that Hannah at least should take some refreshment before their departure. One common-place remark after another had sunk into silence, when Vernon somewhat abruptly asked, "If she knew that orders had been given to fit up the old house for the reception of its owner?"

"I have known it for some days," was the reply. "It will no more be a home suited for a youthful female."

"Certainly not; neither have I the slightest intention of remaining."

"Have you, then, fixed on any future plan?"

"Yes."

"You intend, I suppose, continuing in this neighbourhood?"

Rebecca hesitated. Vernon's hasty temper could no longer bear the curb.

"I might have guessed you would stay: Aubrey de Vere is young and unmarried—no bad chance for an errant princess!" "Stay, Mr. Vernon," interrupted his guest; "do not say what you will soon regret—I am about to depart."

"And whither do you purpose going?"

"To London."

Vernon started from his seat in astonishment—"To London?—to the city of destruction—to the Babylon of the earth—to the sinful and the accursed—where the devil walks abroad, seeking whom he may devour? So young, so friendless, and so fair—you are mad, maiden! mad with sorrow—or pride!"

"I answer to myself—London is the only place where my poor skill in embroidery may find employment; and Hannah has a sister there, with whom we mean to reside."

Vernon walked up and down the room impatiently; at last he stopped before Rebecca, and said, in a voice whose firmness was only preserved by an effort—"Maiden, when I bore you insensible to my house, I thought within myself, that neither by word nor look would I give you cause of annoyance—that I would forbear to urge upon the sacredness of sorrow a suit which that very sorrow makes more earnest. But I cannot, were it only as the daughter of my friend, I cannot see you take a step so rash, so fraught with fatal consequences. Pause, Rebecca, before you depart from my roof. I may not be what your fancy figures; but I love you deeply and truly, and for your sake would change many a habit, perhaps many a fault. I may have been rude, ay harsh, in my speech, but my meaning has been kind. Save your youth from the rough chances of friendlessness and poverty: I offer you an honest name, competence, and an entire heart. We will both make allowances; there will be room in yonder arbour even for your lute; I will study my speech, and watch your look—till our hopes are together, and mutual affection has made our house thrice blessed."

Rebecca felt that the tears were in her eyes, and that her voice was inarticulate; she paused a moment, from a reluctance to give Richard Vernon pain, and she left her hand in his as she spoke. "It may not be, my kind, my only friend: I must alter my very nature ere I could be happy as your wife. Vernon, I dare not marry you."

He flung her hand from him as he caught her words; the long-subdued passion burst at last.

"Accursed be the hour that ever the weakness of my nature led my soul into this folly! Go, and bear with you the bitterness you have infused into my cup; may you know poverty, guilt, sorrow, and shame—may you live to mourn, in sackcloth and ashes, the day you left this roof, never to re-enter it more!—Nay, forgive me!" but Rebecca had quitted the parlour. He made one step to follow her—the next moment he had thrown himself into the huge oaken settle, with his back to the light. The day after, he went to the old house—it was deserted; and he learnt that Rebecca and Hannah had that morning departed for London.

Three years had passed away since Rebecca saw the turrets of the old house recede in the gray mist of early morning; while the drizzling rain, and a low moaning wind, which, even in summer, shook the leaves from the bough, gave to inanimate objects the appearance of a sad farewell. Three years had passed away since Rebecca first watched the shades of evening close on what was but a mockery of daylight—the daylight of a small narrow street in London; and she felt thankful for the obscurity which admitted of a free course to her tears.

I do firmly believe that the Londoner is as contented with his city home as the dweller in the fairest valley among the Appennines; and that habit brings its usual indifference as to place. But to one who has lived all his life in the country, whose path has been through the green field, and bounded only by the green hedge—to whom nothing in the town is endeared by association, and nothing softened by custom, how dreary is the aspect! The confined street, the close air, the dusky atmosphere, the hurrying passengers, the eager and busy yet indifferent faces—all press upon the stranger with an equal sense of discomfort and desolation.

Rebecca's heart died within her as she entered the little dark shop, on her way to the still smaller and darker back-parlour. Three years had been spent in solitude, in poverty, in toil—in all that hardens the heart, and imprints sternness on the brow. Out upon the folly which, in estimating human misery, allows aught to bear comparison with the agony of the poor! I use the word poor relatively; I call not those poor to whom honesty brings self-respect, whose habits and whose means have gone together, and whose industry is its own support. But those are the poor whose exertion supplies not their wants—to whom cold, hunger, and weariness, are common feelings; who have known better days—to whom the past furnishes contrast, and the future fear. The grave may close over the dear and the departed; but in faith there is solace, and in time forgetfulness. The lover may be false to his vow, whose happiness was to have been, like its truth, eternal; yet, after all, the sorrow is purely imaginary, and grief is a luxury in indulgence.

Day by day Rebecca stooped over her embroidery; she debarred herself from rest and food, nay at last encroached even on the Sabbath, which had been held so sacred. The monotony of her existence was only broken in upon by anxiety; she rose early in the morning, and lay down late; still, though bought at the expense of time, youth, and hope, the pittance she could earn was insufficient for their daily wants. In this emergency, it was decided that the two rooms over the shop should be let; though, remote and obscure as was their street, it seemed much easier to decide on letting, than to let these apartments. It so chanced, however, that they succeeded immediately.

Their new resident was a man on whose age it would have been difficult to determine; you might have guessed any period between twenty and thirty; for his slender and almost boyish figure was bent with what might have been either time or infirmity. His hair, of a singularly bright golden hue, was thin, and left exposed a high and strongly marked forehead; his originally fine features were worn to emaciation;

and the mouth was sunken and colourless. His large eyes were of the palest blue, and seemed with the least emotion to fill, as it were, with light—like the flashing and restless brilliancy of sunshine upon water. More richly dressed than suited his circumstances—apparently without a connexion, for none ever came near him—scarcely stirring from home—keeping lonely vigils, that sometimes lasted through the night,—there was obviously a mystery about him; yet it was difficult to hear his sweet low voice, mark his wan and wasted countenance, and believe that the mystery could be in aught evil.

Gradually his gentle and quiet habits led to acquaintance, and acquaintance to confidence. One evening, when Rebecca was sitting working in the little back-parlour, he entered, and turning over the few volumes on her solitary book-shelf, opened one in which was Shakespeare's Midsummer Night's Dream, filled with notes on favourite passages: for before poverty had pressed so heavily, it was Rebecca's delight to write on the margin all she could remember of her father's remarks.

"Ah, this indeed is fame!" exclaimed their visitor, unconsciously soliloquising aloud: "I care not to be bound in scented leather, clasped with the arms of my owner wrought in silver, and to be kept one among many in the ancient library, a thing of show, not of use—a part of the furniture. No; give me the obscure corner and the frequent reading; be mine the few minutes snatched from toil—the one remembered passage which keeps alive the seeds of poetry sown in every heart—the thought that rises remembered in a contemplative hour—the words in which the lover clothes his own love. Ah! the poet hath no true hope, who doth not place it in the many, and in the feeling of the common multitude."

Rebecca now learnt, for the first time, that it was Lee the dramatist who inhabited their dwelling. In a fit of disgust at society, and the excitement produced by the idea of a new work, he had buried himself in entire seclusion, to finish his "Rival Queens."

"I must be by myself when I write," was his frequent observation. "The indifference of my fellow-creatures chills me to the very soul; I feel my own nothingness too severely; I see the selfishness, the vanity, which encircles me, and distrust my own power to animate or to interest: I deeply feel that the people surrounding me are inferior to myself, and I despise their suffrages—I grow vain and mean myself, and am involuntarily actuated by hopes and desires apart from what should be the one sole aim of my existence. I lose my power: I am like a magician who has forgotten the spell by which he once governed the spiritual world. What has the poet to do with the present? Suddenly I feel the shame and misery of such a life; I fly to solitude—I cast the shackles from my hands, the dust from my feet; I think my own thoughts—I dream my own dreams: again the future is to me a great and glorious reward; the feeling rushes to my heart, my lips overflow with music—again the beautiful and the true rise visible before me, and I am happy, very, very happy!"

From that evening he delighted in the society of Rebecca, to whom it was a source of true enjoyment; it was so long since speech had been to her more than the expression of daily regrets and wants—it was as if the higher faculties of her being had lain dormant for a protracted season, and now awoke, as the blossoms on the bough awaken beneath the soft spring rains. Still, she saw with regret that the fiery temper, the excited mind of her companion preyed on his health—the cheek grew paler, the shining eye more restless, every day; and sleep forsook the pillow haunted by fantastic creations. "I know it," he would reply; "and is it a worthy sacrifice that I offer? I believe that the mind may make its own immortality: thought is the spiritual part of existence; and so long as my mind influences others, so long as my thoughts remain behind, so long shall my spirit be conscious and immortal. The body may perish—not so the essence which survives in the living and lasting page."

Sometimes, when weary and desponding,—for who does not despond over even their highest efforts, and feel how little they can paint the beauty and the passion within?—he would come to Rebecca, and ask her to read aloud to him. Her rich sweet voice, her grace of expression, would recall his enthusiasm, and again the "Rival Queens" was resumed with hope and animation. When the task drew near its completion, he told Rebecca that she must insure its success. She looked up inquiringly.

"You must play Roxana."

It little needs to detail the surprise, the various emotions of doubt, hope, and inclination, which were elicited by this remark. Rebecca had that consciousness of talent which must always attend its possession; and she bitterly felt how completely it was now wasted.

Lee's enthusiasm was, as enthusiasm always is, contagious; and when, in his own peculiar manner, he read to her the finished play, the fear of failure became her only fear. Tragedy and actress were presented to Rich, then the manager of the principal London theatre; and both alike met with the most encouraging approval.

Rebecca entered on her new pursuit with all the ardour and all the charm which the imagination lends to its object. Strongly moved and absorbed, she saw in her situation nothing but its poetry. At length the eventful night arrived, and as soon as his heroine stept upon the boards, Lee felt certain of the favourable reception of his drama. The Oriental dress suited well her proud, dark beauty: a crimson turban was folded round her head, ornamented with the plume of that strange bird they call of paradise—both in strong contrast to the raven ringlets which fell in profusion on her flushed cheek. An embroidered robe shewed her exquisite figure, though only the delicate throat and wrist were uncovered; and a veil of silvery tissue partially concealed her profile. Her success was complete. When the first dizzy confusion was merged in the excitement of her part, even Lee himself was satisfied with her conception and execution of it: nothing could be more passionate, more superb, than her revenge; nothing more terrible than the agony of her desertion.

I am persuaded there is no triumph equal to one achieved on the stage—it comes so immediate and so home: you have before you the mass of human beings whose sympathies are at your will; you witness the emotions which you raise, you see the tears which you command: the poet has erected the statue, but it is for you to give it life—the words must find their music on your lips—the generous sentiment, the exalted hope, the touches of deep feeling, ask their expression from you: surely such influence is among the triumphs of the mind, ay and a great and noble triumph. But in this world every thing has its evil; the dust is on the wheels of the conqueror's chariot—the silken-wrought tapestry covers the mouldering wall; and Rebecca soon found that her position was one which often jarred on her imaginative temper. But we make our own path, and fling our own shadow upon it. Never was the lofty purity of her nature more conspicuous than now, when surrounded by so much to which it was utterly opposed.

It was about three months after her first appearance, that two young cavaliers were walking, arm-in-arm, up the Strand, engaged in earnest conversation.

"I tell you," said the youngest, "that it is hopeless."

"I never," replied his companion, "heard of anything so selfish; it is what women always are, but I must say this goes beyond the common allowance—and so our pretty Roxana expects you to marry her!

Wealth, rank—and you are not so bad-looking either, De Vere—pretty well for the Rival Queen!"
"Indeed, Buckingham, you are mistaken; I never saw a creature more unworldly, more disinterested."

"Oh, of course; but it is really too much to have your scruples in addition to hers. However, I pique myself on the impossible. It is matter of conscience, it seems, with your Roxana: well, the chapel in the Savoy is much at your service—I will have it dusted on purpose—and the equerry I recommended has other talents than those of horse-breaking. He lived in my good father-in-law's family to some purpose; his conventicle-drawl is perfection—he will make an excellent priest; and I will give away the bride myself—very generous, when I think how pretty she is!"

A few scruples and a little passing remorse on one side, a sneer and a jest on the other, and the whole affair was arranged.

"You have seen my Roxana for the last time," said Rebecca, about a week after this, to Lee; "you have been too kind a friend to be excluded from my confidence. You will rejoice in my happiness, for happy I must be as the wife of Aubrey de Vere."

"The wife of Aubrey de Vere! you, Rebecca, about to be married?"

He rose from his seat, threw open the lattice, and leant from the window, while his companion stood astonished at the excess of his emotion. Suddenly he turned towards her, while his large shining and melancholy eyes seemed to look into her very heart, and his melodious voice sank on her ear like sad music.

"Rebecca, I have deceived myself—I deemed my heart had but one idol, and my life but one aim; alas, I now find I have one object yet dearer! Alas, my very happiness has blinded me! I have grown so accustomed to see you, to hear you, to refer my every thought to you, that, like the blessed light and air, you have become part of my existence: I cannot, I dare not think of a future without you. Rebecca, you know how earnestly I have laboured for one end—how high, how glorious, I have deemed the poet's calling. Rebecca, there is no honour my ambition could covet that I would not renounce for one smile of yours."

He paused for a moment, and hid his face on the window-sill, while Rebecca stood breathless with distress and surprise. Lee recovered the power of utterance first.

"De Vere—he will be Earl of Oxford—but no—you would not wed only for interest: yet, Rebecca, could we change places, would you still marry him?"

She stood for a moment blushing and irresolute; at length she said in a low but firm voice, "I love himself."

Lee gazed on her earnestly; and to her death Rebecca remembered the wild despair painted on his face. Gently he approached her, and took her hand; his touch was like marble, and contrasted strangely with his flushed and burning cheek.

"Farewell," said he, "last dream of an existence that has been all dreams! I never loved before—I shall never love again. I have often tried to be happy, but in vain; now I have not even an illusion left. Farewell to hope, to honour, to exertion, to poetry—I bid them all farewell, when I say farewell to you."

He dropped the hand which he held—and turned to the door, but languidly, like one who walks in his sleep. Rebecca saw him again, from the window, still moving at the same slow, sad pace. She never beheld him more; and when she next heard of him, it was to learn that he was the inmate of a solitary cell—his fine mind bowed and broken by madness. Awful to know that your soul may depart before yourself!

A cold east wind brought back upon London the smoke of its thousand chimneys. A thick vapour filled the chapel, which the waxen tapers, lighted though it was noon, served rather to shew than to dispel; and Rebecca felt her heart sink within her as she took the offered hand of the Duke of Buckingham, who led her towards the altar. She thought on her extreme isolation from all the ordinary ties of life: others had parents, friends, and relatives; she had none. How utter must be her dependence on Aubrey's love!

His manner, embarrassed and constrained, had nothing in it to reassure her; while Buckingham's gaiety jarred upon her ear, and his jest and flattery were equally unacceptable.

"I have been at merrier funerals," said the Duke of Buckingham, as he turned from the bridal party: "if the mere semblance of the fetters be so melancholy, the Lord have mercy upon those who endure them in reality!"

It was with a mixture of pleasure and pain that Rebecca re-entered the home she had left under such different circumstances; for De Vere had fixed on the old mansion-house for their future dwelling.

"For the present, love, we will live in complete retirement: I care little, while the wonder of our marriage," and he hesitated, "is fresh in men's minds, to endure the questions of the curious, or the comment of the envious."

Rebecca pressed closer to her heart the arm on which she hung; and her silence was more eloquent of happiness than any words. I have ever remarked, that when Fate has any great misfortune in store, it is always preceded by a brief period of calm and sunshine—as if to add bitterness of contrast to all other misery. It is for the happy to tremble—it is over their heads that the thunderbolt is about to burst.

Rebecca lived for a few months in all the deep content of love—every look watched, every thought partaken, her heart was filled with thankfulness and affection. De Vere would sometimes start when he remembered the uncertain tenure of their present state; but conscience, like a child, is soon lulled to sleep; and habit is our idea of eternity. Yet every hour Rebecca became dearer to him; and his few and short absences only brought him to her side with more perfect appreciation and more apprehensive tenderness.

He had now been away for nearly a week, but was expected home that very evening. Who does not know the restlessness of an anticipated arrival? Rebecca wandered from room to room; till at last not even the ingenuity of affection could devise any arrangement or alteration further, that might catch the eye or please the taste of De Vere. It was a lovely afternoon, one of those when autumn atones for the brevity of its days by their beauty; and she walked out, sometimes absorbed in her own thoughts, then again gazing, with a pleasure which half arose from herself, on the country round. Some of the trees yet retained the deep green of their foliage, others wore the brown, purple, and yellow, which, like the bright-hued banners of an army, are the heralds of destruction. A few late flowers were still seen, but their blossoms were fragile and scentless; yet the eye dwelt tenderly upon them—they were the last.

Rebecca had proceeded farther than she had proposed, but the sight of a clump of old yews drew her on—they grew beside her father's grave. More than once she had visited it; and it had cost De Vere his worst pang of remorse, when she pointed out the low grass mound, and said she prayed that her parent's spirit might be gladdened by the knowledge of how happy and how beloved was the child he had left a friendless orphan. It may be a superstition, but it is a grateful and a kindly one, which deems that the righteous dead watch over those they cherished in their pilgrimage on earth. Rebecca knelt beside the grave, but shrunk back—for at that instant a dark shadow fell upon it; she looked up, and saw the harsh and haggard face of Richard Vernon.

"Back, lost and guilty one!" said he, pushing her aside with no gentle hand; "pollute not with your wretched presence the churchyard of your God, and the grave of your father. You mocked at my words when I prophesied of shame, and, lo! it has come upon you. Away!—as the servant of Him whom you have forgotten, I forbid you to remain in this sacred place!"

Rebecca turned towards him with anger, which even her pity could not subdue.

"I know not," said she coldly, "by what right you forbid the wife of a De Vere to approach the church his fathers built; but I leave it; for I would not further unkindness should pass between us."

"Verily, this audacity passeth belief! I know, Rebecca, how you have mingled with the light and the profane; I know how, of your own will, you cast in your lot with the ungodly; I heard too, only three days ago, in yonder accursed Babylon, how Aubrey de Vere had carried off the fair actress to be his paramour;—and yet you dare speak across your father's grave with a lie in your mouth! Wretched girl, kneel—but in sackcloth and ashes—for the sake of him whose dust is at your feet—repent, Rebecca Clinton!"

"Nay," interrupted his auditor, "call me not by a name which I no longer bear. Were it only mine own credit that was touched, I might patiently abide your words; but I may not stay to hear such slander cast upon a true and honourable gentleman, upon my husband."

Before he could reply, she had passed on. His first impulse was to follow her; but as he marked her rapid steps, he desisted, and remained gazing on her lessening figure till lost in the distance, with an expression in which bitterness and sorrow were singularly blended. Rebecca had scarcely reached home, when she received an urgent petition from one of the servants, that she would visit what the doctor, who awaited her arrival, said was his deathbed. She was somewhat surprised at the vehement terms in which the request was couched, for the man declared he could not die in peace till he had seen his mistress.

"Perhaps," thought she, "he leaves one behind him friendless, helpless, even as my father left me—such desolation shall fall on none that I can aid." She entered the large airy room which she had herself ordered to be prepared for him when first seized with sickness; and dismissing the nurse, took her place by the pillow of the dying man. It was the equerry who had personated the clergyman at her marriage! Short and terrible was the narrative to which she had to listen: she spoke not, she moved not—but, pale and cold, sank back in the arm-chair.

"Great God, I have killed her!" shrieked the penitent.

His voice recalled her to herself. She rose, and turning to the bed, stretched her hand towards the emaciated creature who lay there in all but the agonies of death: "I forgive you, and pray God to forgive you too; make your peace with Heaven. May the pardon I yield to you be extended also to myself!"

She went down stairs directly to the laboratory, where De Vere sometimes amused a leisure hour with chemical experiments, and taking from one of the shelves a small phial, hid it in her bosom, and proceeded to her chamber.

"I am going to be fanciful in my dress tonight," said she to her attendant. Her long dark hair was loosened from its braids into a profusion of drooping ringlets; she bound the crimson shawl around her temples; and again assumed the embroidered robe in which De Vere had first seen her. The toilette finished, she flung herself on a pile of rich cushions in the library, to await his arrival; and at that instant he entered—having come through the garden on purpose to surprise her.

"My beautiful masquerader, I must leave you often," said he, tenderly, "if you are to grow so much more lovely in my absence."

And lovely indeed did she look at that moment. We have before remarked that the Oriental style of dress was peculiarly well adapted to the character of her face and figure, and the passionate flush of her cheek gave even more than their usual brightness to her radiant eyes. Aubrey deemed it was delight at his return, and hastened to heap before her the many precious gifts he had brought.

"I did not forget my sweet friend in the hurry of London. Your throat is the whitest, dear one," said he, as he hung round her neck a string of precious pearls.

Supper was now brought in, and Aubrey smiled to see how carefully his favourite dishes had been provided.

"I am not hungry," said Rebecca; "but I will not talk to you now;" and taking up her lute, she began to play, and sang a few simple notes rather than words.

"You have been librarian too," exclaimed Aubrey: "I see all my scattered volumes have been collected: why, what should I do without you?"

"You would miss me?" and laying aside the lute, she came and rested her head on his shoulder, at the same time taking the phial and drinking its contents.

"Miss you, dearest!—how wretched, how inexpressibly wretched should I be without you!"

"I am glad of it!" she cried, springing from her kneeling and caressing attitude, and flinging down the phial, which broke into atoms. "Do you see that? its contents were poison, and I have drank it—drank it even in your very arms! I know all, De Vere—your false marriage, your mock priest. You thought it but a jest to dishonour and to destroy one who trusted you so fondly, so utterly. Go find another to love you as I have done! You planned inconstancy from the first, when I most believed in your love. Well, a little while, and you are free!"

She fell back in a paroxysm of bodily agony, and hid her face in the cushions, but De Vere saw her frame writhe with torture. Suddenly she started up—"I cannot bear it—give me water, for the love of Heaven!"

Her exquisite features were distorted, the blue veins were swollen on her forehead, and her livid lips were covered with froth: again she dashed herself on the ground, and her screams, though smothered, were still audible.

De Vere hung over her in anguish scarce inferior to her own; his call for assistance brought the attendants, and with them the physician, who had just left the chamber of death above. "It is hopeless!" said he, in answer to Aubrey's frantic questions; "no skill on earth could counteract a poison so deadly, and taken, too, in such quantity."

Gradually the convulsions became less violent, and De Vere bore her in his arms to a sofa by the open window. The cool air seemed to soothe her, and she lay for a few moments perfectly passive: the work of years had been wrought upon her sunk and ghastly features. Slowly she raised her head, and put back the thick tresses that pressed upon her brow; she drank the wine the doctor offered, and her recollection returned.

"Aubrey," whispered she, and suffered her head to rest upon his bosom, "my own, my only love, forgive me,"—but her voice failed as she spoke: again a frightful change passed over her face—De Vere held a corse in his arms.

EXPERIMENTS OR, THE LOVER FROM ENNUI

Cecil Forrester was heir to many misfortunes, being handsome, rich, high-born, and clever. His father said it was a shame such a fine fellow should be coddled—took him out to hunt, and gave him port-wine after dinner: his mother said it was a pity such a sweet boy should be spoilt—heaped cushions on his favourite sofa, and perfumed for him a cambric handkerchief with l'esprit de mille fleurs. His father died—his mother was inconsolable for six months, and then married again. Cecil was sent to Eton, where, instead of others indulging him, he indulged himself.

His education was finished by terms at college and seasons in London; and his twenty-second year found him without a pleasure, and without a guinea. The next spring he lived on ennui and credit. He disliked trouble, because he never took it; and he said things and people were tiresome and bores, till he firmly believed it. His feelings were never called forth, his talents never exercised; his natural superiority only served to make him discontented. He saw the waste of his life, but he lacked motive for change: his early habits were those of indolence; and being neither poor nor vain, he had no stimulus to alter them. He did a great many foolish things, regretted them, and did them over again.

One day, after driving in the Park, and wondering why so many people drove there, he turned homewards to dress for a late dinner at the Clarendon. Giving his boy the reins, he resigned himself to meditation,—how unpleasant it was for the pedestrians of Piccadilly to hurry through the mud!—when he was interrupted by the boy's, "Sir, if you please," said in a tone of self-exertion, as if a great deal of mental energy had been collected for its utterance; then, in a deprecatory whisper, "you won't collar me and throw me out of the cab before I've said half, will you?"

"No, I will not," said Cecil.

To make our story shorter than the miniature groom's, he learnt that his own property in himself was in danger; and that, if the patriot's definition of liberty be true—"it is like the air we breathe, without it we die"—his life was near its termination. A writ was issued against him; and, thanks to a douceur to his valet, two professional gentlemen, as he left his toilet, would deprive his friends at the Clarendon of his company.

"I wish I had spoken to my uncle sooner; but, hang it! it is so unpleasant speaking: I'll write."

Forrester was just now in that part of Piccadilly where the White Horse of our Saxon ancestors has degenerated from the banner of a sea-king to the sign of a cellar for taking places and parcels. Still, even as of yore, it hangs over a most migratory multitude. "For Putney, ma'am?" "For Richmond, sir?" One coachman snatches up a child for Turnham Green, while another pops its mamma off to Camberwell. On one side, lemons are selling for a shilling a dozen; on the other, oranges for sixpence. One man blows a horn in your ear, and offers you the Standard; another exerts his lungs, and shews you the Courier. Pencils are to be had for a penny; and penknives, with from three to six blades each, for eighteen pence a-dozen. A fellow with a trunk turns its corner on your temples; another deposits a box, with the grocery of a family—sugar, soap, candles, and all—on your toes. A gigantic gentleman nearly knocks you down in his hurry; and an elderly Jew slips past you so neatly, that you tumble over him before you are aware. Everybody is always too late, and therefore everybody is in a bustle. Two policemen keep the peace; and half-a-dozen individuals, whose notions on the law of property are at variance with established principles or prejudices, attend for the purpose of breaking it. Add to these some females with shawls and sharp elbows; and pattens, whose iron rings are for the benefit of foot-passengers. Such is the White Horse Cellar, and the pavement from Dover Street to Albemarle Street.

Several coaches seemed to be just setting off.

"I will leave London at once," said Forrester. "Do you drive home—you know nothing about me. You are a fine little fellow; I shall not forget you."

So saying, he threw him two or three sovereigns, and got into the first coach. The boy took the money, drove the cabriolet to the stable, and ate and drank himself into a fever, out of which his mother had to nurse him.

Cecil opened his eyes on the grey sea-mist of a Brighton morning. Summer and Brighton!—the vicinity was dangerous. In all probability his tailor would be taking two-penny worth of pleasure on the pier; and if, like John Gilpin's wife, "though on pleasure he was bent," he should also "have a frugal mind," and keep an eye to business, that eye would inevitably fall on him. However, a temporary stay was necessary, for all the personal property he possessed was a handkerchief. Money supplies every want, and he had drawn his last from the banker's the day before. He did not mean to have stirred from his room, but seeing an acquaintance from the window, he resolved to ask him to dinner.

He knew Ravensdale was in love, therefore stupid; still, any company was better than his own. They dined together; and, as a companion is generally the straw that decides an idle man, he set out with him that evening for Hastings. There Mr. Ravensdale expected to meet "the beauteous arbiter who held his fate;" but some slight cause of delay had prevented, and would prevent for a short time, her family's arrival. Cecil quite envied the lover his disappointment—it so entirely occupied him.

A week passed away while he was making up his mind what he should say to his uncle, whose heir he was, and whose kindness he believed would be very likely to assist him; but long before the week was finished, he was quite convinced that Hastings was the most tiresome place on the whole sea-coast. Oh, la peine forte et dure of idleness! Blessed is the banker's clerk, who on a November morning takes his nine-o'clock walk to business under a green umbrella, digesting the memory of his buttered roll and the anticipation of his desk! Blessed is the fag of fashions and fancies, who unrolls ribands from morn till night at Dyde's and Scribe's! Blessed is Mr. Martin, when, transgressing his own act, he urges along the heavy animal on which he perambulates in pursuit of an overladen donkey! Blessed were all these in comparison with Cecil Forrester, "lord of himself, that heritage of wo!"

It was a wet morning, and he loitered at the breakfast-table, though he had long finished both meal and appetite. At length he rose, took two or three turns up and down the room, opened a book, then threw it aside:—(by the by, parents have a great deal to answer for who do not early give their children a taste for reading—novels.) He next approached the window, and proposed to his companion, who was letter-writing, to bet on the progress of two rain-drops. Not having been heard, he proceeded with his cane to trace his name on the damp glass; and at last, in desperation, exclaimed, "How devilish lucky you are, Ravensdale, to be in love! Nothing like love-letters for filling up a rainy morning. A mistress gives a man such an interest in himself! You cannot run your fingers through your hair, without a vision of the locket wherein one of your curls reposes on the fairest neck in the world. An east-wind only conjures up a host of "sweet anxieties;" and if the worst comes to the worst, you can sit down and write sonnets to your inamorata's eyebrow. I have made up my mind—I will try and fall in love. Well, who is there here?"

"Lady de Morne, doing dolorous and disconsolate— only walks in her garden; to be sure, it overlooks the high-road."

"What, a widow! warm or cold, which you will, from the kiss of a dead man! I should taste clay upon her lips!"

"Miss Acton, then, the heiress—utile et dulce."

"No; she belongs to the romantic school, and expects you to rise in the morning to bring her violets with the dew on them; takes country rambles, which would spoil my complexion; and moonlight walks, which would give me cold. Charles Ellis told me that, in a fit of despair occasioned by a run of ill-luck at écarté, he entered into her service for three weeks. He, however, soon found himself feverish—lost his appetite—had a hectic cough—and the fourth week retired on a consumption. I do not feel equal to the exertion,"

"Mrs. Ellerby's two daughters."

"Yes, and never know which is which! I hate people cut out by a pattern. Besides, the only papers in the family are pedigrees; and I am not rich enough to keep a cook, a confectioner, and a wife. Moreover, Mrs. Ellerby, being what is called serious, would expect my attentions and intentions to be as serious as every thing else in the house. No; I want to find some unsophisticated being whose hair curls naturally."

"Now, in pity spare me the description of that never-to-be-discovered perfection, an ideal mistress! Be sure you will fall in love with the very opposite."

"I don't care, so long as I could fall in love. But the rain is over: you will not ride, will you?"

Cecil Forrester rode along the beach by himself. Most earnestly did he wish that some of the young ladies who were sketching "that beautiful effect of light on the grey rocks," would tumble into the water. He might have rushed to the rescue, and so lost his heart in the most approved fashion. Gradually he turned into the very road which he had taken every day, only because he had taken it first. There, as usual, he overtook the same respectable brown coat and horse, and their no less respectable proprietor, whom he regularly encountered. A sudden shower drove them simultaneously under an oak.

English people, as a foreign traveller mentions in his diary, never speak, excepting in cases of fire or murder, unless they are introduced. The old oak did this kind office for the riders.

"The country wanted rain, sir," observed the elderly gentleman.

Forrester felt that his companion had violated every rule of civilised society in thus addressing him; still, he was good-natured, and, moreover, was tired of himself. He therefore replied—"And we are likely to have enough now."

"Ay, ay; it never rains but it pours. I must say I have great faith in Moore's Almanac; it said we should have rain a week ago."

It is needless to detail how acquaintance deepened into intimacy. Silence maketh many friends. The old gentleman took quite a fancy to Cecil, pronounced him such a steady young man, and asked him to dinner.

Forrester went; his host had two daughters—one rather pretty and pensive, the other very pretty and lively. The next week was quite endurable as to length: Cecil copied verses into the eldest Miss Temple's album, and held some green silk for the younger to wind.

The Saturday following his introduction it was a beautiful moonlight evening, and Miss Temple was walking up and down the lawn; she really looked very well, and Cecil was about to join her, when a light step, close beside him, announced her sister.

"'The moon is bright on Helle's wave,
As on that night of stormy water,
When Love, who sent, forgot to save
The young, the beautiful, the brave.'

Even as Love forgot the lover, I have forgot the poet—not a line more can I remember; but I would wager the purse whose green silk I am knitting, and which you helped me to wind, against its weight in green grass, that those very lines are in Mary's head at this minute."

"Why those lines especially?"

"Oh, dear! now, cannot you guess?—why, everybody knows!"

"But as I am not everybody, I shall not know till you tell me."

"Oh, but really I shan't tell you!"

"Oh, but really you must!"

"To be sure, there is not a neighbour but is aware that she is engaged to such an interesting young man now in Greece. But, dear, dear! you must have noticed how she coloured up when you talked about a turban's suiting her style of face. And did you observe my father's laugh at dinner, to-day, when he asked her if she liked Turkey?"

"And so Miss Temple has got a lover—and I need not ask if you have one also."

"Not I indeed—dear, if I had a lover one week, I should forget him the next!"

Somehow or other the dialogue ended in one or two pretty speeches—the last things in the world to particularise. And Forrester went home quite convinced that Elizabeth was far the prettiest of the two, and bound by promise to accompany them the next night to a fancy ball in the neighbourhood.

Now, a fancy ball is bad enough in London, where milliners are many, and where theatres have costumes that may be borrowed or copied; but in the country, where people are left to their own devices—truly to them may be applied the old poet's account of murderers, "their fancies are all frightful." Miss Temple, we need scarcely observe, wore a turban, and looked as Oriental, at least as un-English, as possible. Elizabeth preferred going back upon the taste of her grandmothers; and when Cecil first saw her standing in the window, with the loose hanging sleeves of former days, and floating draperies of an antique striped silk—her pretty arms just bare to the elbow, and her fair hair in half-dishevelled curls,—he decided, that if you are very young and pretty, extravagance in costume carries its own excuse.

To the dance they went: the dancing was bad, the music worse, and instead of ice, sago was handed round to keep the young people from taking cold. Yet Cecil had passed worse evenings. We talk of unsophisticated nature—I should like to know where it is to be found. Elizabeth Temple's hair did curl naturally—she made her own dresses—and for accomplishments, played on her grandmother's spinnet by ear, knitted purses, and took the housekeeping alternate weeks with her sister;—yet had she talents for flirtation at least equal to those of any young lady whose dress and accomplishments are the perfection of milliners and May Fair. Cecil was her partner the most of the evening; and, by a few ingenious and invidious parallels, implied not expressed, between him and the other cavaliers,—that preference of attention, the best of feminine flattery,—and a deference to his opinion, nicely blended with a self-consciousness of prettiness, Elizabeth contrived to keep him rather pleasantly awake. Mr. Temple's house lay in his way home; and though he had already ate supper enough for six months, his friends would make him go in for another. On his departure, Elizabeth gave him some trifling commission at Hastings; and while she was writing it down, Forrester, with that universal habit of the idle, took up whatever happened to be near, in the laudable intention of twisting it to pieces. It was the little green silk purse, and he looked on it with a remembrance of the slender fingers he had seen employed in its making. Could he be mistaken? no, he saw the letters distinctly, C. F. worked in light brown hair—his own initials; and he now recollected that Miss Temple had asked him the other morning what was his Christian name; on hearing which, she made the usual remark of young ladies in such cases, "Dear, what a beautiful name!"

Elizabeth, turning round at this minute, saw the purse in his hand, and also which of the stitches had fixed his attention. Blushing even deeper than the occasion required, she said in a low but hurried voice, "I really cannot have my work spoilt; give me the purse, Mr. Forrester."

"Never!" said Cecil, in what was for him a very energetic tone.

"Oh, but I must and will have it!" making an attempt to snatch it from him—to which his only answer was to catch her hand and kiss it.

"Elizabeth, my dear, Mr. Forrester must be tired; do not detain him with your foolish commissions," said her father, who advanced, and himself accompanied his guest to the hall, taking leave of him with a mysterious look of mingled cordiality and compassion.

The young gentleman rode home, too tired for anything but sleep; and when he arose the next morning, it was with a conviction that light brown hair was "an excellent thing in a woman." True, in a fit of absence, while debating whether or not he should write to his uncle before he rode out, he dropped the purse into the fire; nevertheless his vexation at the incident was sufficiently flattering to its maker. As soon as he had decided that he would put off writing till the next day, he ordered his horse and rode to Mr. Temple's. In the hall he caught a flying glance of Elizabeth, whose fair face was evidently much disfigured with recent crying. Lord Byron says,

"So sweet the tear in beauty's eye,
Love half regrets to kiss it dry."

Now we, on the contrary, hold that a good fit of crying would, for the time, spoil any beauty in the world.

Cecil entered the parlour somewhat abruptly; Mrs. Temple was saying, "I do so pity the poor young man." On what account the "poor young man" was pitied, Forrester's entrance prevented his learning, for she instantly broke off her speech in great confusion.

Mr. Temple paced up and down the room, as if he thought exercise a great relief to anger. Both received their visiter with even more than their usual kindness, but with obvious and painful embarrassment. Husband and wife interchanged looks when the topic of the weather was exhausted, each seemingly expecting the other to speak. A few minutes passed in silence—at length Mr. Temple began.

"I am truly sorry—"

"My dear," interrupted his wife.

"I am sure you will be very glad—"

"Nay," again rejoined the lady, "it is presuming too much on Mr. Forrester's kindness to suppose that he will take an interest in our affairs."

Mr. Forrester hastened to assure her he took the very warmest.

"My daughter Elizabeth," said the old gentleman.

"Good heavens!" thought Cecil, "he is not going to ask me what my intentions are! I am sure I can't tell him."

"My daughter Elizabeth,"—how the words were bolted out!—"is going to be married."

"My dear, how could you be so abrupt?" ejaculated the lady.

As if to give his visiter time to recover the shock, Mr. Temple went on rapidly, "To a son of a very old friend of mine—Charles Forsyth—you saw him last night— very fine young man; he made her an offer this very morning, before breakfast."

"My love, you need not be so particular."

Forrester, who, to tell the truth, had no stronger feeling on the subject than surprise—perhaps a little mortification—now offered his congratulations. Not being very desirous of encountering the fair fabricator of the deceiving initials, the betrothed of Mr. Charles Forsyth, he took the first opportunity of making his bow and his exit.

"Poor young man, how well he has behaved!" said the mother.

"I knew he would'nt take it much to heart," answered the father.

As Cecil passed through the hall, he heard Elizabeth's voice tuned to rather a petulant key.

"In spite of all mamma says about feeling, and papa about principle, and you with your devoted affection to one object, I can't see the great harm of a little innocent flirtation—Mr. Forrester won't break his heart for passing an evening more pleasantly than he would otherwise have done; and if I had not flirted with him, Charles Forsyth, though he is the son of my father's old friend, would not have made his offer these six months—and one cannot wait for ever, you know."

"Very true," muttered Cecil Forrester, as the hall-door was closed after him. That evening he wrote to his uncle; and passed the intermediate time in cutting his name on the table, and wondering what would be the reply. He received an answer by return of post—angry and yet kind, requesting his immediate presence in town. He made a farewell call at Mr. Temple's—saw Elizabeth and Mr.Charles Forsyth in an arbour at the end of the garden, making love—thought they would soon be very tired— and bade the rest of the family goodbye, who thought he looked pale. Mrs. Temple for a fortnight afterwards read every article headed "Interesting Suicide," in the newspapers; and though they were all "interesting," they did not interest her. Cecil arrived at his uncle's, who commenced the conversation by declaring he would cut him off with a shilling, and ended by paying his debts and making him an allowance. The next week saw two different announcements in the Morning Post—one was the marriage of Elizabeth Temple to Charles Forsyth, Esq.; the other the departure of Mr. Cecil Forrester for Naples.

A friend had offered to take him thither in his yacht, and for that reason only he had gone. Of course he ascended Vesuvius—visited churches, pictures, statues, &c.; but, alas! these are tastes which require cultivation—and at present they appeared to Cecil in the light of duties. Not speaking the language of the country, he was excluded from all enjoyment of Italian society, and English he had entered an inward protest against. Two friends had refused to cash a draft for him: one because he could not, the other because he would not—one from inability, having no money to spare; the other from principle, as he made it a rule never to lend. A lady, with whom he had been quite l'ami de famille, with four pretty daughters, had actually avoided seeing him in the Park before it was known that his uncle intended arranging his affairs. Cecil was therefore persuaded of the heartlessness of artificial society. Still, he had no innocent beliefs in rural unsophistication—Elizabeth Temple had cured him of any such vain fancies: he retained a predilection for the natural—only he decided that it was not to be discovered in any civilised country. He used to sit on the sea-shore, and spend the evening poring over some volumes of Lord Byron he had found by accident, and in throwing pebbles into the sea. A beautiful dream of a Circassian had been floating on his mind, when the arrival of the Dey of Algiers with his harem at Naples changed his reverie to absolute reality.

One fine morning, a whole array of palanquins, the forms within them shrouded from human eye, passed him on his ride—the next day the same—the third the curtains of one slightly moved, a sprig of jasmine was thrown out, and the day following one of myrtle. That night Cecil read Lord Byron—the Giaour and the Corsair were only interrupted by Lalla Rookh. He went to bed, and dreamt of the maids

"Who blushed behind the gallery's silken shades."

The next day he began to study Arabic, and to endeavour to find some means of conversing with this unknown Houri. To be sure, there were curtains, locks, bolts, bars, and cimeters; still,

"Love will find its way
Through paths where wolves would fear to prey;
And if it dares enough, 'twere hard
If passion met not some reward:"

and Cecil succeeded in establishing an intercourse with this Haidee of his fancy, by means of a petty officer in the Dey's retinue, who contrived to bribe one of the slaves in immediate attendance on the harem, from whom he learnt that she was the last and loveliest purchase of his lord. The progress of love-affairs is usually very rapid, and this was no exception to the general rule. A plan of escape was soon organised; her especial guardian agreed to facilitate her remaining after dusk in the garden, which was bounded by a river; a few planks would form an easy communication with the water; a boat might be stationed there; and four good rowers would convey them in half an hour to a little villa, which Cecil, in a week's whim for solitude, had rented: once there, no trace would be left of their flight, and no fear remain of discovery. The night fixed on found them punctual to their appointment—so were the slave and the beautiful Georgian. The zeal of Sidi Mustapha, the first agent, was quite wonderful; he sprang up the boards to aid the lady's descent, and would scarcely allow Cecil to give himself any trouble in the matter, till it was evident she could not get down without help from both. After some effort, she and her drapery—the quantity of which seemed enormous—were deposited in the boat. They arrived in silence and safety at the villa: Sidi and Forrester supported their prize into the saloon, fear seeming to have deprived her of the power of motion; and the Algerine hastened to discharge the boatmen with all possible caution. Every thing had been prepared; the table was covered with the richest sweetmeats, the rarest perfumes, the most aromatic coffee. Cecil's impatience was now at its height.
"Gulnare!"—but she replied not:—"dear Gulnare!"

Suddenly he recollected that she might perhaps not understand Arabic—at all events, his Arabic. Still, till his interpreter returned, it would be but civil to help her off with the large blue veil, or mantle, which entirely covered her. Politely proffering his assistance, he removed her veil, and flung it on a chair near.

The scream which followed this act astonished him far less than the discovery to which it led. The lovely Georgian was so fat, that it was with the greatest difficulty she could stand; and an exquisitely tattooed wreath of hyacinths, of a fine blue, began at her chin, meandered over her cheeks, and covered her forehead.

"Oh!" ejaculated Cecil, "if I had but profited by my reading! Why did I not sooner remember the traveller I studied in the days of my youth, who said that in the East a beauty was a load for a camel!"

At this moment Mustapha re-entered the saloon.

"O Allah, how beautiful! By the head of the Prophet, she is a rose—a full moon!"

Cecil sprang forward, with the true Englishman's impulse, to knock him down. Ill-timed admiration is enough to enrage a saint. The shrill cries of the lady, however, diverted his attention.

"Unless you wish me to be deafened outright, do learn the cause of her horrible clamour."

"Your highness has taken off her veil."

"Which, for my own sake, I shall return as speedily as possible."

Without a moment's delay he restored the screen and quiet at the same time; and with the aid of Mustapha supported the fair slave to a pile of crimson satin cushions, which had been collected for her especial use.

"And now, in the name of the devil, what shall I do with her?"

Sidi seemed a little surprised at the question, and forthwith began a string of Arabic verses about this star of the morning, this pearl of the world, this rose of a hundred leaves, which the stranger was fortunate enough to possess. Well, to make the best of a bad bargain, and short of a long story, he married the Georgian to Sidi Mustapha.

After all, Englishmen are patriotic with partridges before their eyes; and this little adventure gave Cecil an excuse for returning to England before September. What is the reason that we find it so satisfactory to make excuses to ourselves—the only persons in the world to whom they must be altogether needless?

It was the last week in August when he reached the Abbey, his uncle's seat. How advantageously did the luxurious foliage of the thickly leaved woods, as yet untouched by one tint of autumn, and the bright green grass of the fields, contrast with the parched and sultry aspect of the southern summer he had left behind! It was long—in youth, everything seems long—since he had felt a sensation of pleasure so keen as he experienced when the tall oaks of the avenue closed over his head. The rooks were gathering to their rest, as noisily as children; but the old and familiar are ever soothing sounds. In the distance he could see the slim and mottled deer sauntering lazily along in the full enjoyment of security; and the last red flush of evening was reflected in a large piece of water, which glittered through the dense branches.

At length he arrived in the court, where half-a-dozen gray-headed serving-men came out to meet "Master Cecil," as they persisted in calling him. It is very agreeable to have people glad to see you, even if there be no better reason for their joy than that they knew you as a child. A spaniel now put its nose into his hand: but the dog's memory was more faithful than that of its master; for the visitor had some difficulty in recognising, in the heavy and feeble creature that claimed his notice, the once slight and agile partner of his boyish amusements.

"My poor Dido! can this be you?"

"All my young mistress's care," said one of the servants. At this moment the young mistress herself appeared, and Cecil found that he had forgotten her as much as his dog. He had left her a pale, sickly, even plain child: she had sprung up into a bright, blushing, and most lovely girl. Her flaxen hair had darkened into a rich chestnut; and the only trace of "little Edith" was in the large blue eyes, which remained the same. Cecil was quite surprised that she so instantly remembered him; but five years after twenty do not make the difference they do before that age.

Sir Hugh was as glad to see his nephew as a gentleman of the old school always is on the stage; and in half an hour the trio were comfortably situated in the library—some dinner ordered for Cecil—an extra bottle of port for the old gentleman—and Edith, seated on a low stool at her father's knee, was quite delighted when the conversation went back to their childish sports, and what a pet the poor little delicate child used to be of her cousin's.

The next month flew away imperceptibly. Cecil listened patiently to the politics of the Morning Post—for Edith read them aloud to her father. He also found that he could read at his young hostess's work-table; then he was so very useful in the flower-garden, which was especially hers; there were, besides, visits to the gold and silver pheasants, long rides over the heath, long walks through the forest, and long evenings, when Sir Hugh sat by the fire-side and slept, and Edith sung sweet old ballads to her harp. The result of all this was inevitable: had it been in a melodrame, the young people could not have fallen more desperately in love. Let others talk of the miseries of the tender passion, Cecil was eloquent on its comforts: he had never been so occupied or so amused before.

On the 1st of October, a bright clear morning, when the few flowers that still linger on sunny terrace or southern nook are in all that glow of gorgeous colouring which so peculiarly belongs to autumn, the young lady of the Abbey stept out on the balustrade to pluck the last buds of the Provence rose. A few late geraniums and myrtles were yet beautiful and green; but suddenly Edith turned and gathered from a luxuriant plant its only cluster of orange flowers. They suited well her array, for Edith was that day garbed as a bride. The glossy brown hair—that golden brown which shines on the pheasant's wing—fell in large curls from her white wreath, half-hidden by the long veil; the white satin dress had no ornament—not a gem marred its rich simplicity. She leant pensively on a corner of the marble pilaster: for she stood now on the threshold of youth; she was about to put away childish things, to take upon her higher duties; and her destiny was given—how utterly!—into the hands of another. Already the shadow of love deepened the seriousness of that graceful brow. Still, she was only leaving the home of her childhood for a time, not as the young bride often leaves that home—for ever. To wed with Cecil was but giving Sir Hugh another child.

"Come, Edith mine!" said a sweet voice at her side; and the lover led her to her father.

In another half-hour the bells were ringing cheerfully on the air; and during the many years that the old Abbey was gladdened with their mutual happiness, Cecil never felt inclined to go to Hastings from ennui, or to Naples as an experiment; but found ample employment and content around his own home, and by his own hearth.

AN EVENING OF LUCY ASHTON'S

The autumn wind swung the branches of the old trees in the avenue heavily to and fro, and howled amid the battlements—now with a low moan, like that of deep grief; now with a shrill shriek, like that of the sufferer whose frame is wrenched by sudden agony. It was one of those dreary gales which bring thoughts of shipwreck,—telling of the tall vessel, with her brave crew, tossed on the midnight sea, her masts fallen, her sails riven, her guns thrown overboard, and the sailors holding a fierce revel, to shut out the presence of Death riding the black waves around them;—or of a desolate cottage on some lone sea-beach, a drifted boat on the rocks, and the bereaved widow weeping over the dead.

Lucy Ashton turned shivering from the casement. She had watched the stars one by one sink beneath the heavy cloud which, pall-like, had spread over the sky till it quenched even that last and lovely one with which, in a moment of maiden fantasy, she had linked her fate.

"For signs and for seasons are they," said the youthful watcher, as she closed the lattice. "My light will soon be hidden, my little hour soon past."

She threw herself into the arm-chair beside the hearth, and the lamp fell upon her beautiful but delicate face, from which the rose had long since departed; the blue veins were singularly distinct on the clear temples, and in the eye was that uncertain brightness which owes not its lustre to health. Her pale golden hair was drawn up in a knot at the top of her small and graceful head, and the rich mass shone as we fancy shine the bright tresses of an angel. The room was large, lofty, and comfortless, with cornices of black carved oak; in the midst stood a huge purple velvet bed, having a heavy bunch of hearse-like feathers at each corner; the walls were old; and the tapestry shook with every current of passing air, while the motion gave a mockery of life to its gaunt and faded group. The subject was mythological—the sacrifice of Niobe's children. There were the many shapes of death, from the young warrior to the laughing child; but all struck by the same inexorable fate. One figure in particular caught Lucy's eye; it was a youthful female, and she thought it resembled herself: the outline of the face certainly did, though "the gloss had dropped from the golden hair" of the pictured sufferer. "And yet," murmured Lucy, "far happier than I! The shaft which struck her in youth did its work at once; but I bear the arrow in my heart that destroys me not. Well, well, its time will come!"

The flickering light of the enormous chimney, whose hearth was piled with turf and wood, now flung its long and variable shadows round the chamber; and the figures on the tapestry seemed animate with strange and ghastly life. Lucy felt their eyes fix upon her, and the thought of death came cold and terrible. Ay; be resigned, be hopeful, be brave as we will, death is an awful thing! The nailing down in that close black coffin—the lowering into the darksome grave—the damp mould, with its fearful dwellers, the slimy worm and the loathsome reptile, to be trampled upon you—these are the realities of dread and disgust! And then to die in youth—life unknown, unenjoyed; no time to satiate of its pleasures, to weary of its troubles, to learn its wretchedness—to feel that you wish to live a little longer—that you could be happy!

"And," added the miserable girl, "to know that he loves me—that he will kneel in the agony of a last despair by my grave! But no, no; they say he is vowed to another—a tall, dark, stately beauty:—what am I, that he should be true to me?"

She wrung her hands, but the paroxysm was transitory; and fixing her eyes on the burning log, she sat listlessly watching the dancing flames that kept struggling through the smoke.

"May I come in, Miss Ashton?" said a voice at the door; and, without waiting for an answer, an old crone entered. She approached the hearth, placed in a warm nook a tankard of mulled wine and a plate of spiced apples, drew a low and cushioned settle forwards, seated herself, and whispered in a subdued, yet hissing tone, "I thought you would be lonely, so I came up for half an hour's chat: it is the very night for some of your favourite stories."

Lucy started from her recumbent position, cast a frightened glance around, and seemed for the first time sensible of her companion's presence.

"Ah! is it you, Dame Alison? sooth it is but a dreary evening, and I am glad of a companion—these old rooms are so gloomy."

"You may well say so, for they have many a gloomy memory; the wife has wept for her husband, and the mother for her child; and the hand of the son has been against his father, and that of the father against his son. Why, look at yonder wainscot; see you no dark stains there? In this very room—"

"Not of this room; tell me nothing of this room," half screamed the girl, as she turned from the direction in which the nurse pointed. "I sleep here; I should see it every night:—tell me of something far, far away."

"Well, well, dear; it is only to amuse you. It shall not be of this room, nor of this house, nor even of this country; will that please you?"

Lucy gave a slight inclination of the head, and again fixed her gaze steadily on the bright and sparkling fire; meantime the old woman took a deep draught from the tankard, disposed herself comfortably in her seat, and began her story in that harsh and hissing voice which rivets the hearing whereon it yet grates.

THE OLD WOMAN'S STORY.

"Many, many years ago there was a fair peasant—so fair, that from her childhood all her friends prophesied it could lead to no good. When she came to sixteen, the Count Ludolf thought it was a pity such beauty should be wasted, and therefore took possession of it: better that the lovely should pine in a castle than flourish in a cottage. Her mother died broken-hearted; and her father left the neighbourhood, with a curse on the disobedient girl who had brought desolation to his hearth, and shame to his old age. It needs little to tell that such a passion grew cold—it were a long tale that accounted for the fancies of a young, rich, and reckless cavalier; and, after all, nothing changes so soon as love."

"Love!" murmured Lucy, in a low voice, as if unconscious of the interruption: " Love, which is our fate, like Fate must be immutable: how can the heart forget its young religion?" "Many," pursued the sibyl, "can forget, and do and will forget. As for the Count, his heart was cruel with prosperity, and selfish with good fortune; he had never known sickness which softens—sorrow which brings all to its own level—poverty which, however it may at last harden the heart, at first teaches us our helplessness. What was it to him that Bertha had left the home which could never receive her again? What, that for his sake she had submitted to the appearance of disgrace which was not in reality her's?—for the peasant-girl was proud as the Baron; and when she stept over her father's threshold, it was as his wife.

"Well, well, he wearied, as men ever weary of woman's complaining, however bitter may be the injury which has wrung reproach from the unwilling lip. Many a sad hour did she spend weeping in the lonely tower, which had once seemed to her like a palace; for then the radiance of love was around it —and love, forsooth, is something like the fairies in our own land; for a time it can make all that is base and worthless seem most glittering and precious. Once, every night brought the ringing horn and eager step of the noble hunter; now the nights passed away too often in dreary and unbroken splendour. Yet the shining steel of the shield in the hall, and the fair current of the mountain spring, shewed her that her face was lovely as ever.

"One evening he came to visit her, and his manner was soft and his voice was low, as in the days of old. Alas! of late she had been accustomed to the unkind look and the harsh word.

"'It is a lovely twilight, my Bertha,' said he; 'help me to unmoor our little bark, and we will sail down the river.'

"With a light step, and yet lighter heart, she descended the rocky stairs, and reached the boat before her companion. The white sail was soon spread; they sprang in; and the slight vessel went rapidly through the stream. At first the waves were crimson, as if freighted with rubies, the last love-gifts of the dying Sun—for they were sailing on direct to the west, which was one flush, like a sea of blushing wine. Gradually the tints became paler; shades of soft pink just tinged the far-off clouds, and a delicate lilac fell on the waters. A star or two shone pure and bright in the sky, and the only shadows were flung by a few wild rose-trees that sprang from the clefts of the rocks. By degrees the drooping flowers disappeared; the stream grew narrower, and the sky became darker; a few soft clouds soon gathered into a storm: but Bertha heeded them not; she was too earnestly engaged in entreating her husband that he would acknowledge their secret marriage. She spoke of the dreary solitude to which she was condemned; of her wasted youth, worn by the fever of continual anxiety. Suddenly she stopped in fear—it was so gloomy around; the steep banks nearly closed overhead, and the boughs of the old pines which stood in some of the tempest-cleft hollows met in the air, and cast a darkness like that of night upon the rapid waters, which hurried on as if they distrusted their gloomy passage.

At this moment Bertha's eye caught the ghastly paleness of her husband's face, terribly distinct: she thought that he feared the rough torrent, and for her sake; tenderly she leant towards him—his arm grasped her waist, but not in love; he seized the wretched girl and flung her overboard, with the very name of God upon her lips, and appealing, too, for his sake! Twice her bright head—Bertha had ever gloried in her sunny curls, which now fell in wild profusion on her shoulders—twice did it emerge from the wave; her faint hands were spread abroad for help; he shrunk from the last glare of her despairing eyes; then a low moan; a few bubbles of foam rose on the stream; and all was still—but it was the stillness of death. An instant after, the thunder-cloud burst above, the peal reverberated from cliff to cliff, the lightning clave the black depths of the stream, the billows rose in tumultuous eddies; but Count Ludolf's boat cut its way through, and the vessel arrived at the open river. No trace was there of storm; the dewy wild flowers filled the air with their fragrance; and the Moon shone over them pure and clear, as if her light had no sympathy with human sorrow, and shuddered not at human crime. And why should she? We might judge her by ourselves; what care we for crime in which we are not involved, and for suffering in which we have no part? "The red wine-cup was drained deep and long in Count Ludolf's castle that night; and soon after, its master travelled afar into other lands—there was not pleasure enough for him at home. He found that bright eyes could gladden even the ruins of Rome—but Venice became his chosen city. It was as if revelry delighted in the contrast which the dark robe, the gloomy canal, and the death-black gondola, offered to the orgies which made joyous her midnights."

"And did he feel no remorse?" asked Lucy.

"Remorse!" said the crone, with a scornful laugh; "remorse is the word for a child, or for a fool—the unpunished crime is never regretted. We weep over the consequence, not over the fault. Count Ludolf soon found another love. This time his passion was kindled by a picture, but one of a most strange and thrilling beauty—a portrait, the only unfaded one in a deserted palace situate in the eastern lagune. Day after day he went to gaze on the exquisite face and the large black eyes, till they seemed to answer to his own. But the festival of San Marco was no time for idle fantasies; and the Count was among the gayest of the revellers. Amid the many masks which he followed, was one that finally rivetted his attention. Her light step seemed scarcely to touch the ground, and every now and then a dark curl or two of raven softness escaped the veil; at last the mask itself slipped aside, and he saw the countenance of his beautiful incognita. He addressed her; and her answers, if brief, were at least encouraging; he followed her to a gondola, which they entered together. It stopped at the steps of the palace he had supposed deserted.

"'Will you come with me?' said she, in a voice whose melancholy was as the lute when the night-wind wakens its music; and as she stood by the sculptured lions which kept the entrance, the moonlight fell on her lovely face—lovely as if Titian had painted it.

"'Could you doubt?' said Ludolf, as he caught the extended hand; 'neither heaven nor hell should keep me from your side!'

"And here I cannot choose but laugh at the exaggerated phrases of lovers: why, a stone wall or a steel chain might have kept him away at that very moment! They passed through many a gloomy room, dimly seen in the moonshine, till they came to the picture-gallery, which was splendidly illuminated—and, strange contrast to its usual desolation, there was spread a magnificent banquet. The waxen tapers burned in their golden candlesticks, the lamps were fed with perfumed oil, and many a crystal vase was filled with rare flowers, till the atmosphere was heavy with fragrance. Piled up, in mother-of-pearl baskets, the purple grapes had yet the morning dew upon them; and the carved pine reared its emerald crest beside peaches, like topazes in a sunset. The Count and the lady seated themselves on a crimson ottoman; one white arm, leant negligently, contrasted with the warm colour of the velvet; but extending the other towards the table, she took a glass; at her sign the Count filled it with wine.

"'Will you pledge me?' said she, touching the cup with her lips, and passing it to him. He drank it—for wine and air seemed alike freighted with the odour of her sigh.

"'My beauty!' exclaimed Ludolf, detaining the ivory hand.

"'Nay, Count,' returned the stranger, in that sweet and peculiar voice, more like music than language—'I know how lightly you hold the lover's vow!'

"'I never loved till now!' exclaimed he, impatiently; 'name, rank, fortune, life, soul, are your own.'

"She drew a ring from her hand, and placed it on his, leaving her's in his clasp. 'What will you give me in exchange,—this?'—and she took the diamond cross of an order which he wore.

"'Ay, and by my knightly faith will I, and redeem it at your pleasure.'

"It was her hand which now grasped his; a change passed over her face: 'I thank you, my sister-in-death, for your likeness,' said she, in an altered voice, turning to where the portrait had hung. For the first time, the Count observed that the frame was empty. Her grasp tightened upon him—it was the bony hand of a skeleton. The beauty vanished; the face grew a familiar one—it was that of Bertha! The floor became unstable, like water; he felt himself sinking rapidly; again he rose to the surface—he knew the gloomy pine-trees overhead; the grasp on his hand loosened; he saw the fair head of Bertha gasp in its death-agony amid the waters; the blue eyes met his; the stream flung her towards him; her arms closed round his neck with a deadly weight; down they sank beneath the dark river together—and to eternity."

THE STORY OF HESTER MALPAS

There is a favourite in every family; and, generally speaking, that favourite is the most troublesome member in it. People evince a strange predilection for whatever plagues them. This, however, was not the case with Hester Malpas. The eldest of six children, she was her father's favourite, because from her only was he sure of a cheerful word and a bright smile. She was her mother's favourite, because every one said that she was the very image of that mother herself at sixteen. She was the favourite of all her brothers and sisters, because she listened patiently to all their complaints, and contributed to all their amusements; an infallible method, by the by, of securing popularity on a far more extended scale.

Mr. Malpas was the second son of a prosperous tradesman in Wapping,—a sickly child. Of course, he shrank from active amusement. Hence originated a love of reading, which, in his case, as in many others, was mistaken for a proof of abilities. Visions of his being a future lord chancellor, archbishop of Canterbury, or at least an alderman, soon began to stimulate the ambition of the little back-parlour where his parents nightly discussed the profits of the day, and the prospects of their family. The end of these hopes was a very common one;—at forty, Richard Malpas was a poor curate in Wiltshire, with a wife and six children, and no chance of bettering his condition. He had married for love, under the frequent delusion of supposing that love will last under every circumstance most calculated to destroy it; and, secondly, that it can supply the place of everything else. Many a traveller paused to admire the beauty of the curate's cottage, with the pear-tree, whose trained branches covered the front; and the garden where, if there were few flowers, there was much fruit; and which was bounded on one side by a green field, and on the other by the yet greener churchyard. Behind stood the church, whose square tower was covered with ivy of a hundred years growth. Two old yews overshadowed the little gate; and rarely did the sunset glitter on the small panes of the Gothic windows without assembling half the children in the hamlet, whose gay voices and ringing laughter were in perfect unison with a scene whose chief characteristic was cheerfulness. But as whoso could have lifted up the ivy would have seen that the wall was mouldering beneath; and whoso could have looked from the long, flower-filled grass, and the glad and childish occupants of the rising mounds, to the dust and ashes that lay perishing below; so who could have looked into the interior of that pretty cottage would have seen regret, want, and despondency. Other sorrows soften the heart,—poverty hardens it. Nothing like poverty for chilling the affections and repressing the spirits. Its annoyances are all of the small and mean order; its regrets all of a selfish kind; its presence is perpetual; and the scant meal, and the grudged fire, are repeated day by day, yet who can become accustomed to them? Mr. and Mrs. Malpas had long since forgotten their youth; and if ever they referred to their marriage, on his part it was to feel, too late, what a drawback it had been to his prospects, and to turn in his mind all the college comforts and quiet of which his ill-fated union had deprived him. Nor was his wife without her regrets. A woman always exaggerates her beauty and its influence when they are past; and it was a perpetual grief to think what her pretty face might have done for her. As the children grew up, discomfort increased; breakfast, dinner,—supper was never attempted,—instead of assembling an affectionate group, each ready with some slight tale of daily occurrence, to which daily intercourse gives such interest, these meals were looked forward to with positive fear. There was never quite enough for all; and the very regret of the parents took, as is a common case, the form of scolding. When Hayley tried Serena's temper, he forgot the worst, the real trial—want; and want, too, felt more for others than for yourself. The mother's vanity, too,—and what mother is without vanity for her children?—was a constant grievance. It was hard that hers should be the prettiest and worst-dressed in the village. In her, the distress of their circumstances took the form of perpetual irritability,—that constant peevishness which frets over everything; while in Mr. Malpas it wore the provoking shape of sullen indifference.

In the midst of all this, Hester grew up;—but there are some natures nothing can spoil. The temper was as sweet as if it had not breathed the air of eternal quarrellings; the spirits as gay as if they had not been tried by the wearing disappointment of being almost always exerted in vain. She had ever something to do—something to suggest; and when the present was beyond any actual remedy, she could at least look forward; and this she did with a gaiety and an energy altogether contagious. Everybody has some particular point on which they pique themselves; generally something which ill deserves the pride bestowed upon it. Richard Malpas particularly prided himself on never having stooped to conciliate the relations, who had both felt, and very openly expressed, the anger of disappointed hope on his marriage. His brother had lived and died in his father's shop: perhaps, as his discarded relative formed no part of his accounts, he had forgotten his very existence. On his death, shop and property were left to his sister Hester; or, as she was now called, Mrs. Hester Malpas. After a few years, during which she declared that she was cheated by everybody,—though it must be confessed that the year's balance told a different story every Christmas,—she sold her interest in the shop, and, retiring to a small house in the same street, resolved on making her old age comfortable. It is very hard to give up a favourite weak point; but to this sister Mr. Maples at length resolved on applying for assistance;—he had at least the satisfaction of keeping the step a secret from his wife. Hester was his confidant,—Hester the sole admirer of "his beautiful letter." Hester put it in the post-office; and Hester kept up his hopes by her own; and Hester went every day, even before it was possible an answer could arrive, to ask, "Any letter for my father?" for Mr. Malpas, fearing, in spite of his sanguine confidant, the probability of a refusal, had resolved that the letter should not be directed to his own house. Any domestic triumph, that the advice of writing, so often urged, had been taken too late, was by this means averted.

The day of the actual return of post passed, and brought no answer; but the next day saw Hester flying with breathless speed towards the little fir-tree copse, where her father awaited her coming. She held a letter in her hand. Mr. Malpas snatched it from her. He at once perceived that it was double, and post-paid. This gave him courage to open it, and the first thing he saw was the half of a bank-note for twenty pounds. To Hester this seemed inexhaustible riches; and even to her father it was a prodigious sum. For the first time she saw the tears stand in his eyes.

"Read it, child," said he, in a broken voice. Hester kissed him, and was silent for a moment, and then proceeded with her task. The hand-writing letters rather resembled the multiplication-table than the alphabet. The epistle ran as follows:—

"Dear Brother,—Received yours on the 16th instant, and reply on the 18th; the delay of one post being caused by getting a Bank of England note. I send one half for safety, and the other will be sent to-morrow. They can then be pasted neatly together. I sha'n't go back to old grievances, as your folly has been its own punishment. If people will be silly enough to marry, they must take the consequences. You say that your eldest daughter is named after me. Send her up to town and I will provide for her. It will be one mouth less to feed. You may count on the same sum (twenty pounds) yearly. I shall send directions about Hester's coming up, in my next letter.

"Your affectionate sister, Hester Malpas."

Poor Hester gasped for breath when she came to her own name. Even her glad temper sank at the bare idea of a separation from her parents.

"Me, father!" exclaimed she; "oh! what will my mother say?"

"No; as she always does to anything I propose," said her father.

To this Hester made no reply. She had long felt silence was the only answer to such exclamations. For once, like her father, Hester dreaded to return home. "Is it possible," thought she, "we can be taking so much money home so slowly?" and she loitered even more than her father. Hester had yet to learn that no earthly advantage comes without its drawback. At length the silence was broken, and Hester listened with conviction, and a good fit of crying, to the many advantages her whole family were to derive from her adoption by her aunt. Still, "What will my mother say?" was the only answer she could give.

When we expect the worst, it never happens. Mrs. Malpas caught at the idea of Hester's going to town with an eagerness which inflicted on poor Hester the severest pang she had ever known. "And is my mother so ready to part with me?" was a very bitter thought. Still, if she could have read that mother's heart, she would have been comforted. It was the excess of affection that made the sacrifice easy. All the belief in the sovereign power of a pretty face,—all the imagination which Mrs. Malpas had long ceased to exercise for herself,—were exerted for her daughter. Like all people who have lived their whole life in the country, she had the most unreal, the most magnificent ideas of London. Once there, and Hester's future fortune was certain. Besides, she had another reason, which, however, from the want of confidence which ran through the whole family, she kept to herself. There was a certain handsome youth, the son of a neighbouring farmer, between whom and Hester she thought the more distance the better. She had suffered too much from a love-match herself to entertain the least kindness towards such a step. The faults we ourselves commit are always those to which we are most unforgiving. Hester herself had never thought about what the feeling was which made her blush whenever she met Frank Horton. No girl ever does. It was shyness, not deception, that made her avoid even the mention of his name. The word love had never passed between them. Still the image of her early playmate was very frequent amid the regrets with which she regarded leaving her native place. The next day brought the second letter from Mrs. Hester Malpas. It contained the other half of the bank-note; and as it never seemed to have crossed the good lady's mind that there could be an objection to her proposed adoption, she had made every arrangement for her journey the following week. She had taken her place in the coach, stated her intention of meeting her at the inn, and hoped that she worked well at her needle. There was little preparation to be made. Her aunt had said, "that she could come with only the clothes on her back," and she was taken very nearly at her word.

The evening before her departure, she went for a solitary walk, lingering amid all her old favourite haunts. Her spirits were worn out and dejected. It jarred cruelly upon her affectionate temper to find that her absence was matter of rejoicing to her whole family. The children, naturally enough, connected Hester's departure with the new indulgences, the result of their aunt's gift; and childhood is as selfish from thoughtlessness as age is from calculation. Her parents merged in the future that present which weighed so heavily upon poor Hester. She was stooping, with tearful eyes, to gather some wild flowers in the hedge, when Frank Horton, who had joined her unperceived, gathered them for her.

"And so, Hester, you are going to London, and will soon forget all your old friends." Hester had no voice to assure him that she should not. Her silence gave her companion the better opportunity of expressing his regrets, doubly touching to the affectionate girl, who had just been thinking that her departure was lamented by no one. Hester's heart was so full of love and sorrow, that it was impossible for some not to fall to his share; and they parted, if not with a positive promise, yet with a hope that their future life would, in some way or other, be connected together.

It was a sleepless night with the young traveller; and she awoke from a confused dream, which blended together familiar objects in a thousand fantastic combinations. She wakened up suddenly, and the first object on which her eyes opened was her mother,—the mother she had thought almost unkind,—seated weeping by the bedside. Not all Mrs. Malpas's brilliant visions of the future could console, when it came to the actual parting. She bent over the fair and innocent face which looked so child-like asleep, in an agony of fear and love. To-morrow, and the music of that ready footstep would be silent in their house,—to-morrow, and those sweet eyes would no more meet her own with their peculiar bright, yet watchful look. A little corded box was on the floor; she turned away from it, and burst into tears. It was the last suppressed sob that had roused her daughter. In a moment Hester was up, and weeping on her mother's neck; and yet, sad as were the tears, they were pleasant when compared with those with which she had cried herself to sleep.

It was later than they had supposed; and the sound of the church clock striking five made them start; and Hester, with a trembling hand, began to dress. In half an hour the London coach would pass, and there were some fields between them and the high-road. This last half hour showed Hester how truly she was beloved. The youngest child neglected the breakfast; and while her father pressed her to eat, he could not eat himself. All felt movement a relief,—all accompanied her to the gate where they were to wait for the coming stage. They had scarcely reached the road, when the guard's horn was heard in the distance. The coach appeared,—it stopped,—Hester took her place behind,—and dizzy with the rapid and unaccustomed motion. The little group, that stood watching, swam before her sight. Still she saw them, and she did not feel quite alone. Tears shut them out,—she took her handkerchief; it was raised scarce an instant, but a rapid turn in the road shut them out from her lingering and longing gaze.

The guard, under whose especial charge she had been placed, did his best to console her; but found the attempt vain, and as he had children of his own, thought it all very proper that a daughter should cry at parting with her parents. He left her to the full indulgence of her tears. Nothing could well be more dreary than the journey was to poor Hester. The bright morning soon clouded over, and a small, drizzling rain covered every object that might have diverted her attention, with a thick, dull mist. Such a sad and monotonous day leaves nothing to tell; and Hester found herself bewildered, cold, tired, hungry, and wretched, in the inn-yard where the coach stopped. Such a scene of confusion had never before met her sight; and she stood hopeless and frightened precisely in the place where the guard had helped her to alight, without an idea, or even a care, of what would happen to her next. She was roused by someone at her elbow inquiring "for the young woman that Mrs. Hester Malpas expected;" and in a moment the guard had consigned her to the care of a stranger. It was a neighbour whom her aunt had sent to meet her. Mr. Lowndes asked her how she did, received no answer, made up his mind that she was stupid and shy, considered that to talk was no part of his agreement with Mrs. Malpas, and hurried along the streets as fast as possible. The noise, the multitude of houses, the haste, the silence, made poor Hester's heart die within her. She felt indeed that she was come to a strange land, and grew more and more wretched at every narrow street through which they passed. At length her conductor stopped at a door. Hester started at the sound of the knocker. She was astonished at her guide's audacity in making such a noise, though, Heaven knows, it was but tame, meagre sort of rap after all.

"I have brought your niece safe," said Mr. Lowndes; "and good night in a hurry."

"Won't you walk in and have some supper?" said a voice so harsh that it gave an invitation the sound of a dismissal.

"No, no; some other night. I and my mistress will look in together."

Hester was sorry to part with him; she felt so desolate, that even the companionship of half an hour was something like a claim to an acquaintance.

"Come in, child," said the same forbidding voice; and a hand laid upon her arm conducted her into a small but comfortable-looking parlour. The light cheered, the warmth revived, but still Hester could not muster resolution enough to look up.

"Can't the girl speak?"

Hester tried to murmur some inarticulate sounds, but gave up the attempt in despair and tears.

"Poor thing! come. take a seat; you will be better after supper." And the old lady began to bustle about, and scold the servant for not bringing in the supper before it was possible.

"Take off your bonnet."

Hester obeyed; and the readiness with which this slight act was performed, together, perhaps, with the trace of crying very visible on the face, had a favourable effect on her hostess, who parted her hair on her forehead, and said, with much kindness of manner, "Your hair is the colour mine used to be—scarcely, I think, so long;—I used to be celebrated for my head of hair." And the complacency with which the elderly dame reverted to the only personal grace she had ever possessed diffused itself over her whole manner. Hester now looked at her aunt, who was the very reverse of what she had imagined: she had always thought she would be like her father, and fancied a tall, dark, and handsome face. No such thing. Mrs. Hester Malpas was near sixty (her niece had left age quite out of her calculation), and was little, thin, harsh-featured, and of that whole sharp and shrewish appearance so often held to be the characteristic of singlehood. She was, however, very kind to her young guest—only once spoke to her rather sharply for not eating the nice supper which she had provided, observing "that now-a-days young people were so whimsical;" adding, however, immediately afterwards, "Poor thing! I dare say you are thinking of home." She lighted Hester herself to the little room which she was henceforth to consider her own, and bade her good night, saying, "I am a very early person, but never mind about to-morrow morning—I have no doubt you will be very sleepy." And certainly Hester's head was scarcely on her pillow before she was asleep.

Never was change so complete as that which now took place in Hester's life. Nothing could be more dull, more monotonous, than her existence;—the history of one day might serve for all. They rose very early;—people who have nothing to do always make the day as long as possible:—they breakfasted—the same eternal two rolls, and a plate of thin bread and butter. After some time Hester was intrusted with the charge of washing the breakfast-things—a charge of no small importance, considering that her aunt regarded those small china teacups as the apple of her eye: then she read aloud the chapters and psalms of the day—then sat down to some task of interminable needlework—then dinner—then (after a few weeks' residence had convinced Mrs. Malpas that her niece required exercise and might be trusted) she was allowed to walk for two hours—then came tea—the cups were washed again—then the work-basket was resumed—and Mrs. Hester told long stories of her more juvenile days—stories which, however, differed strangely from those treasured up by most elderly gentlewomen, whose memory is most tenacious of former conquests; but the reminiscences in which Mrs. Hester delighted to indulge were of the keen bargains she had driven, most girls, would have listened with all the patience of interest. An unhappy attachment is irresistible to the imagination of eighteen; but with these tender and arithmetical recollections it was impossible for any young woman to sympathise;—however, she listened very patiently—supper came at nine—and they went to bed at ten. Sometimes a neighbour of Mrs. Malpas's own standing dropped in, and everything on the table was, if possible, found more fault with than usual. The truth was that Mrs. Hester Malpas had the best heart and the worst temper in the world, and she made the one an excuse for the other. Hester was grateful, and thought she was content—while her constant attention to her aunt's slightest wish, the unvarying sweetness of her temper, won upon the old woman more than she would have acknowledged, even to herself. She scolded her, it is true, because she scolded every body; but she felt a really strong affection for her, which showed itself in increasing kindness to her family; and scarcely a month passed without some useful present, and which Hester had the pleasure of packing, directing, and sending off by the very coach which had brought herself to London. That dreary and terrible inn-yard was now connected with her pleasanter moments. Still this was but a weary life for a girl of nineteen, and Hester's sweet laugh grew an unfrequent sound, and her bright cheek lost its rich colour. The neighbours said that Mrs. Malpas was worrying her niece to death. This was not true. Mrs. Malpas was both fond of and kind to her niece in her way, and, had she noted the alteration, would have been the first to be anxious about her; but Hester's increasing silence and gravity were rather recommendations, and as to her looking pale, why she never had had any colour herself, and she did not see why her niece should have any—colour was all very well in the country.

A year passed away unmarked by any occurrence, when, one summer afternoon, as Hester was taking her accustomed walk, she heard her name suddenly pronounced. She turned, and saw Frank Horton.

"I have been watching for you," said he, hastily drawing her arm within his, and hurrying her along, "these two hours. I was afraid you would not come out; but here you are, prettier than ever!"

Hester walked on, flurried, confused, surprised, but delighted. It was not only Frank Horton that she was glad to see, but he brought with him a whole host of all her dearest remembrances—all her happiest hours came too—she faltered half a dozen hurried questions, and all about home. Frank Horton seemed, however, more desirous to talk about herself: he was eager in his expressions, and Hester was too little accustomed to flattery not to find it sweet. She prolonged her walk to the utmost, and when they separated, she had promised, first, that she would not mention their meeting to her aunt, and, secondly, that she would meet him the following day. It was with a heavy heart Hester bent over her work that evening. One, two, three days went by, and each day she met Frank Horton; the fourth, as she entered the parlour with her bonnet on, to ask, as was her custom, if her aunt wanted anything out, "No," said Mrs. Malpas, her harsh voice raised to its highest and harshest key, "you ungrateful, deceitful girl! I know what you want to go out for: take off your bonnet this moment, for out of the house you don't stir. Your young spark won't see you for one while, I can tell him."

Mechanically Hester obeyed: she took off her bonnet, and sat down. She knew she had done wrong, and she was far too unpractised in it to attempt a defence. Pale and trembling, she only attempted to conceal her tears. A few kind words, a tone of gentle remonstrance, and Mrs. Malpas might have moulded her to her will; but she was too angry, and reproach after reproach was showered upon the unhappy girl, till she could bear it no longer, and she left the room. Her aunt called her back, but she did not return. This was Hester's first act of open disobedience, and the indignation it excited was proportioned to the offence. Three more miserable days made up the week;—taunts, reproaches of every kind were lavished upon her—and what she felt most keenly was, that every person who came near the house was treated with an account of her falsehood and ingratitude, till at last Mr. Lowndes, the very person who gave the information, could not help exclaiming, "Lord, Mrs. Hester! she is not the first girl who did not tell every time she went out to meet her sweetheart."

If Hester was not the first girl, it would not be her aunt's fault if she was not the last—for not one moment in the twelve hours was there a cessation from the perpetual descant on the heinousness of her offence. On the Saturday night, after she had gone into her own room, the servant girl came up softly, and, giving her a letter, said, "Come, miss, don't take on so—I am sure no good will come of mistress's parting two true lovers; but dear, she never had one of her own—and such a handsome young man—but, Lord! is that her calling?" and the girl darted off, leaving Hester the letter.

A thrill of delight lighted up her pale face as she opened the precious epistle. Under any circumstances, what happiness, what an epoch in existence is the first love-letter!—and to Hester, who would have been thankful to a stranger for one word of kindness, what must not the page have seemed whose every word was tenderness? Frank wrote to say that he knew how she had been confined to the house —that he had kept purposely out of the way—and that he entreated her to meet him as she went to church the following Sunday—that he had something very important to tell her—and that he would never ask her to meet him again. Hester wondered in her own mind whether she should be allowed to go to church—trembled at the idea of thus profaning the sabbath—half resolved to confess all to her aunt—then found her courage sink at the idea of that aunt's severity—read the letter over again—and determined to meet him. She was late the ensuing morning, when Mrs. Hester came into her room, and exclaimed angrily, "So I suppose, as your spark has taken himself off, you do not want to go out? Please to make haste and get ready for church—I am sure you have need to pray for your sins."

Hester had not courage to reply. She dressed; and, after telling her she ought to be ashamed of making herself such a figure with crying, Mrs. Malpas dismissed both her and the servant to church. Very infirm, she herself rarely left the house, but used to read the service in the parlour, which was her sitting-room.

Trembling and miserable, Hester proceeded in the direction indicated by her lover; he was there before her,—and, with scarcely a word, she followed him hurriedly till they reached a more remote street, where, at least, neither were known. As they walked along, half Hester's attention had been given to the bell tolling for church; suddenly it ceased, and the silence smote upon her heart. Never before had she heard that bell cease but within the walls of the sacred edifice.

"Oh pray make haste—what can you have to say?—I shall be so late in church!" exclaimed she, breathless with haste and agitation.

"I shall not detain you again," replied he, in a low and broken voice. "Hester, I could not leave England without bidding you farewell, perhaps for ever!" She clung to his arm. To one who had never made but a single journey in all her life—whose idea of the world was composed of a small secluded village, and a few streets in a dull and said her companion, gazing earnestly and sadly on her pale and anxious face, "I go on board to-day—I cannot stay here—I am off to America—I have done very wrong in renewing my acquaintance with you—but, with all my faults, I do love you, Hester, very truly and dearly. It was hard to leave my native country, and not leave one behind who would say 'God bless you!' when I left—or give me one kind thought when far, far away. I ask for no promise, Hester; but when I return, altered I hope for the better in every way, you will find Hester Malpas has been my hope and my object." She could say nothing—the surprise of this departure overwhelmed every other feeling. She walked with him in silence—she listened to his words, and felt a vague sort of satisfaction in his expressions of attachment and fidelity; but she answered only by tears. Frank was the first to see the necessity of their parting. He accompanied her back to her aunt's, and Hester let herself in, as she had the key of the back door. He followed her into the passage—he clasped her to his heart, and turned hastily away. Hester was not aware that he was gone till she heard the door close after him; she wanted consolation—it would have been a relief to have spoken to any one—she felt half inclined to seek her aunt and confess the meeting, but her courage failed, and she hurried into her own little room, where she was soon lost in a confused reverie which blended her aunt's anger and Frank's departure together.

Leaving her to the enjoyment (as people are said to enjoy a bad state of health) of her solitary and melancholy reverie, we will follow the worthy Mr. Lowndes out of church, who, leaving his wife to hurry home about dinner, declared his intention of paying Mrs. Hester Malpas a visit. The fact was, he had missed Hester from her accustomed place in church—thought that she was still kept prisoner to the house—and considering her to have been punished quite long enough, resolved to speak a word in her favour to her aunt. He knocked at the door, but instead of being let in with that promptitude which characterised all the movements of Mrs. Hester's household, he was kept waiting; he knocked again— still no answer. At this moment, just as Mr. Lowndes' temper was giving more way than the door, the servant girl came up, who had loitered longer on her way from church, arrived, and let them in together. She threw open the parlour door, but instantly sprung back with a scream. Mr. Lowndes advanced, but he, too, started back with an exclamation of horror. The girl caught hold of his arm, and both stood trembling for a moment, ere they mustered courage to enter that fated and fearful room. The presence of death is always awful, but death, the sudden and the violent, has a terror far beyond common and natural fear. The poor old lady was lying with her face on the floor, and the manner of her death was instantly obvious—a violent blow on the back of the head had fractured the skull, and a dark red stain marked the clean large arm-chair, the customary seat of the deceased. "Good God! where is Miss Hester?" exclaimed Mr. Lowndes. The servant girl ran into the passage, and called at the foot of the stairs—she had not courage to ascend them. There was at first no answer—she called again—the door of Hester's apartment was opened slowly, and a light but hesitating step was heard. "Miss Hester, oh!

Miss Hester, come down to your aunt." Hester's faint and broken voice answered, "Not yet, not yet—I cannot bear it."

Fatally were these words remembered against her. That evening saw the unfortunate girl confined in a solitary cell in Newgate. We shall only give the brief outline of the evidence that first threw, and then fixed the imputation of guilt upon her. It was evident that the murderer, whoever he was, had entered by the door: true, the window was open, but had any one entered through it there must have been the trace of footsteps on the little flower-bed of the small garden in front. The house, too, had been rifled by one who appeared to know it well, while nothing but the most portable articles were taken—the few spoons, the old lady's watch, and whatever money there might have been, for not a shilling even was to be found anywhere. A letter, however, was found from Mr. Malpas to his sister, mentioning that Frank Horton, who had long been very wild, had been forced to quit the neighbourhood in consequence of having been engaged in an affray with some gamekeepers, and it was supposed that poaching was the least crime of the gang with whom he had been connected. The epistle concluded by a hope very earnestly expressed, that if, as common report went, Frank had gone up to London, he might not meet with Hester, and begging if he attempted to renew the acquaintance, a stop should be put to it at once. It was proved that Hester had met this young man several times in secret, the last in defiance of her aunt's express prohibition; that instead of going to church she had met him, and he had been seen leaving the house with all possible haste about the very time the murder had been committed, and he was traced to the river side. Two vessels had that morning sailed for America, but it was impossible to learn whether he was a passenger in either. Hester's own exclamation, too, seemed to confirm every suspicion, so did her terror, her confusion, and her bewildered manner. Everybody said that she looked so guilty, and the coroner's inquest brought in a verdict for her committal.

It was a fine summer evening when Mr. Malpas and his family were seated, some in the porch of the cottage, while the younger children were scattered about the garden. There was an expression of cheerfulness in the face of the parents very different to the harsh, hard despondency of a twelvemonth since; and Hester, as her mother always prognosticated she would, had indeed brought a blessing on her family. Many an anxious glance was cast down the road, for to-day the post came in, and one of the boys soon discovered running at full speed, and a letter was in his hand. "It is not my sister's handwriting," said he, with the blank look of disappointment. Mr. Malpas opened the epistle, which was from Mr. Lowndes, and broke kindly, though abruptly, his daughter's dreadful situation. The unhappy father sunk back senseless in his seat, and in care for his recovery Mrs. Malpas had a brief respite,—but she, too, had to learn the wretched truth. How that miserable day passed no words may tell. Early next morning Mr. Malpas woke from the brief but heavy sleep of complete exhaustion; the cold grey light glared in from the window—he started from his seat, for he had never gone to bed—it was but a moment's oblivion, for the whole truth rose terrible and distinct. In such a state solitude was no relief, and he sought his wife to consult with her on the necessity of his going to London. He found only his other daughter, who had scarcely courage to tell him that her mother had already departed for town, and to give him the few scarcely legible lines which his wife had left.

The next evening, and Mrs. Malpas had found her way to the cell of her unhappy child. All was over— she had been tried and found guilty, not of the actual murder, but of abetting and concealing it, and the following morning was the one appointed when the sentence of the law was to be carried into effect. "This is not Hester!" exclaimed Mrs. Malpas, when she entered the cell: and even from a mother's lips the ejaculation might be excused, so little resemblance was there between the pale emaciated creature before her, and the bright and blooming girl with whom she had parted. Hester was seated on the side of the iron bedstead—her hands clasping her knees, rocking herself to and fro, with a low monotonous moan, which would rather have seemed to indicate bodily pain than mental anguish. Her long hair—that long and beautiful brown hair of which her mother had been so proud—hung dishevelled over her shoulders, but more than half of it was grey. Her eyes were dim and sunk in her head, and looked straight forward, with a blank stupid expression. Her mother whispered her name—Hester made no answer; she took one of her hands—the prisoner drew it pettishly away. That live-long night the mother watched by her child—but that child never knew her again. After some time she seemed soothed by those kind and gentle caresses, but she never gave the slightest token of knowing from whom they came.

Morning arrived at last. With what loathing horror did Mrs. Malpas watch the dim grey light mark the dull outline of the grated window! The morning reddened, and as the first crimson touched Hester's face as it rested sleeping on her mother's shoulder, somewhat of its former beauty came back; to that fair young face. She slept long, though it was a disturbed and convulsive slumber. She was roused by a noise in the passage—bolt and bar fell heavily; there was the sound of many steps—strange dark faces appeared at the door. They came to take the prisoner to the place of execution! The men approached Hester—they raised her from her seat—they bound her round childish arms behind her. The mother clung to her child, but that child clung not in return. Mrs. Malpas sunk, though still retaining her hold, on the floor. With what humanity such an office permitted, they disengaged her grasp—they bore away the unresisting prisoner—the door closed, and the wretched mother had looked upon her child for the last time.

It was about a twelvemonth after the execution of Hester Malpas that the family were seated again, on a fine summer evening, round the door of their cottage; but a dreadful alteration had taken place in all. The father and mother looked bowed to the very earth—the very children shrunk away if a stranger passed by. Mr. Malpas had inherited his sister's property, much more considerable than had ever been supposed; but though necessity forced its use, he loathed it like a curse. An unusual sight now—the postman was seen approaching—he brought Mr. Malpas a newspaper. He shuddered as he took it, for he knew Mr. Lowndes's handwriting again. He opened it mechanically, and a large "read this" directed his attention to a particular paragraph. It was the confession of a Jew watchmaker, who had just been executed for burglary; and, among other crimes, he stated that he was the real murderer of Mrs. Hester Malpas, for which a young woman, her niece, had been executed. He had entered the window by means of a plank thrown from the garden railing to the casement, when with one blow he stunned the old lady, who was reading. Mr. Malpas went no further—the thick and blinding tears fell heavily on the paper— he could not read it aloud, but he put it into his wife's hand, with a broken ejaculation, "Thank God, she was innocent!"

The facts of the Jew committing the murder, and the old lady's niece being hanged, are perfectly true. It happened in Wapping some forty years since.

THE HEAD

PART I

The Countess Amalie de Boufflers was one of the very prettiest specimens of a pretty woman that Paris and nature had ever constructed. She had bright golden hair, always exquisitely dressed, whether sprinkled with powder, lighted with diamonds, and waving with feathers, or suffered to hand in the studied negligence of a crop à l'Anglaise. She had a hand as white as a lily, and nearly as small; a foot and ankle as faultless as the satin slippers—which their artist said required the imagination of a poet to conceive, and the genius of a sculptor to execute: her walk was the most exquisite mixture of agility and helplessness that ever paid a cavalier the compliment of attracting his attention and requiring his aid; her dancing made the Prince de Ligne exclaim, "I understand the fables of mythology—Madame realizes the classic idea of the Graces." Never did anybody dress so exquisitely; Raphael himself never managed drapery to such a flow of elegance, Corregio never understood half so well the arrangement of colours, and in the management of fan, flacon, scarf, handkerchief, and bouquet she was unrivalled—"the power of science could no further go." Beautiful she was not, for the imagination and the heart must enter into the composition of beauty—that beauty which is both poetry and passion; but, after all, there is no word in French that translates our "beautiful," and who in her own sphere could have desired her to be what their language did not even express? Numberless were the lovers whom she drove to despair—and many were those whom she did not! But all her petites affaires de coeur were arranged in the most perfect taste; no scenes, no jealousies, no brouilleries; these are things which a femme d'esprit always avoids, and, as the Countess was wont to observe, "Je suis femme d'esprit par la grâce de Dieu—et je le sais."

It was amazing, in spite of all her avocations, how much she contrived to do for her husband: half at least of his pensions, places, and favours were owing to her solicitations; and this was very disinterested—for as they scarcely ever met, she had no motive for keeping him in good humour. Talk of the industry of the lower classes:—no woman with two cows, six children, to say nothing of pigs and poultry, and who takes in washing to boot, ever worked harder than the Countess de Boufflers; the poets whom she patronised; the plays which she protected, for a smile from the fair face bending anxiously from the box above, and meeting his gaze, quite by chance, disarmed many a stern young critic in the parterre;—then the fashions which she invented; the financiers' wives whom she put in the way of spending their husbands' money creditably, i. e. as quickly and as uselessly as possible; her assiduous attendance at court and at mass; her thousand and one balls; her myriad of letters and notes, and, above all, the inimitable suppers, of which she was the presiding deity; the piquant things which she said, the charming things which she looked, and the innumerable things which she did, proved, at least, that if idleness be the mother of mischief, she carefully avoided the parent, whatever she might do to the child.

Time past on as lightly as he always steps over flowers, Brussels carpets, marble terraces, green turfs, or whatever simile may best express a path without an impediment. Every day added one to the crowd of her adorers—people feel so safe in an admiration which is general; to think with others is the best plan of never committing yourself—the unsupported opinion runs such risks. But Fate is justly personified as a female, in so many caprices does she indulge; and one malicious fancy which she contrived was exceedingly displeasing to la belle comtesse. One night her husband entered her boudoir; a surprise disagreeable on many accounts, but most disagreeable in its consequences. With that perfect ease which constitutes perfect good breeding, he announced that an affair of honour forced him to leave the court for a while, and madame must be ready to accompany him to his chateau by daybreak. Amalie was horror-struck: she could have been so interesting miserable about the count's misfortune—so useful in arranging matters: such an opportunity for general sympathy might never occur again; but though she had not had many experiences of the kind, yet one or two instances of a divided opinion convinced her, that when M. le Comte did make up his mind, like the laws of the Medes and Persians, it was not to be changed, and, it must be confessed, with no better reason. There is nothing in nature so impracticable as the obstinacy of your true husband; it is the insurmountable obstacle—the Alps no female vinegar can melt. Amalie knew her destiny, and submitted to it with as good a grace as she could. "Grace," as she afterwards observed, "is a duty which a woman owes to herself on all occasions." The count thanked her, kissed her hand, and bowed out of the room, leaving her to console herself as she could, and Amalie rarely wanted the means of consolation. We will only notice two principal sources; first, she had some rustic or rather romantic notions about innocent pleasures, interesting peasants, sheep, and roses growing in the open air; secondly, it was a great relief to think of the sensation her absence would produce; she had quite comforted herself while she reflected on les misérables whom she would leave behind; she also felt a little touch of curiosity when the count desired her company; she became almost interested about him while thinking what could be the cause. It was but a little mystery, scarcely worth penetrating, if she had known all. De Boufflers was himself in despair at leaving Paris, and was only induced to take so rash a step from considering that his own chateau was preferable to the Bastile. In an agony of anticipated ennui he looked about for a resource; his wife's evil genius managed that her idea should occur to his mind. Everybody said she was so charming, would not her company be better than none at all—or, worse than none at all—his own? The Comte de Boufflers was himself "the ocean to the river of his thoughts," and he decided that it was far better for half the salons in Paris to be desolés than to omit even so slight a precaution as his wife's company, when reduced to sixty miles from Paris, tapestried chambers, some fifty worm-eaten portraits, and an avenue with a rookery.

The next morning Amalie, who had made up her mind to enact la femme comme il y en a peu, was ready, and they drove off rapidly, after a conjugal dispute as to whether both her pet poodle and paroquet were to have a place in the carriage; but, as is usually the case in trifles, female supremacy carried the day. For many miles the countess was kept awake by hope and reflection; the hope, a sort of vague, romance-reading hope, that some adventure would fall out by the way, and the reflection on the despair which her sudden departure would occasion. At length her imagination and her temper were alike exhausted; she became sleepy and petulant, and, if such a term could be applied to any form of speech proceeding from a mouth whence spring had copied its roses (we merely translate into prose an expression in the last copy of verses addressed to the divine Amalie), she actually scolded, her poodle barked and snapped, her paroquet screamed and bit, and when they arrived at the end of their journey, the count was plunged in a profound meditation as to what other people could find so fascinating in his wife.

The chateau was, like the general run of chateaux left to a concierge and one or two old retainers, as dilapidated as their dwelling. A ghost had taken possession of one chamber—smoke of a second—a murder, ages ago, had been in a third—and a fourth swarmed with rats. The count sought refuge in shooting partridges from morning till night, and the countess in despair and letter-writing. There is such a thing as friendship, for her epistles received answers full of condolences, regret, and, dearer still, news. One letter, however, from l'amie intime, Madame de Bethune, made her feel almost as desperate as people do when they tear their hair, drown themselves, pay their debts, or commit any very outrageous extravagancy. The precious yet cruel scroll gave a full and particular account of a late fête at Marli. Marie Antoinette had decided on a taste for rural and innocent pleasure, and the whole court had grown rural and innocent to a degree. Nothing was to be seen but crooks, garlands, straw hats, and "white frocks with broad sashes," quite English: then they had a real-earnest mill and a boat, and the gardens were filled with groups enacting rustic scenes. It was enough to provoke a saint—though Amalie made no pretensions to such a character, whatever she might to that of an angel—to have everybody else playing at a country life, while she was acting in reality. But the worst was yet to come; the part selected by the queen herself for "sa belle Amalie" had of necessity been given to Madame de Mirvane, "who," pursued her informant, "looked pretty enough, but managed the dove, which she was to sit beneath a tree caressing, with no sort of grace. How differently would it have been perched on your mignon fingers! it was dreadful that such an interesting part, so simple and so tender, should have been so utterly wasted; but this will make her majesty still more in earnest about obtaining M.de Boufflers' return. What business has notre bon homme Louis with a gentleman's affair of honour?" The only consolation which the countess could devise was to try how the new and simple costume would suit her; she could at least have the satisfaction of her own approval. The next day saw her seated beneath an old tree in the neglected garden, through whose boughs the sudden sunshine fell half green, half golden, as the light of the noon and the hue of the leaf mingled together. Her hair was carelessly combed back under a wide black chip hat, with just un nœud du ruban; she wore the simplest of white dresses; and, as no dove could be procured, her paroquet was fastened with a silken string, and placed in an attitude on the prettiest hand in the world. But, alas! projects fail, strings break, and birds fly away, even from such a jailer as la belle Amalie; suddenly the slender fastening gave way, the paroquet spread its wings, and was soon lost amid the branches. In such a case there is but one resource, and the countess executed a most musical shriek; this being of no avail, "tears were in the next degree;" but the countess had no idea of wasting such interesting things as tears on herself, so she was returning to the chateau for assistance to recover her fugitive, when a rustling amid the boughs overhead attracted her attention, and the next moment a singularly handsome young man sprang to the ground and presented her bird. "Ah, perfide!" exclaimed Amalie, overwhelming her favourite with caresses—upon principle—for affection is the sign of a good heart, and simplicity was not only so engaging, but in such exact keeping with her costume! "But I am quite ungrateful with delight," turning to the young stranger, who was gazing upon her with evident admiration; and raising, but for a moment only, her eyes to his face, "I really know not how to thank you enough."

"Ah, madame," exclaimed the youth, "I am but too fortunate," and he stopped, embarrassed, but reluctant to depart:—the countess had no intention that he should.

"How could you," continued she, glancing, with a slight shudder, at the old chestnut tree, from which he had just descended, "trust your life amid these decaying branches? Ah, even my attachment to ce pauvre chéri is a selfish pleasure;" and, lost in the terror her fancy had conjured up, and the philosophic reflexion it had inspired, Amalie seated herself on a projecting root, whose moss was beautiful enough to have been an artificial covering. The stranger stood at a little distance, and even Amalie felt something very like confusion at his earnest and prolonged gaze; for hommage she was always prepared, but sincerity took her a little by surprise—however, the novelty made the affair more piquante. "Monsieur does not belong to these parts?" Now there was insinuated flattery in this negative method of putting the question; it was as much as to say, it was impossible they could have produced him.

"I am a native of the adjacent valley."

"Strangers alike upon our native soil, I suppose?" said Amalie.

"I have passed the greater portion of my life here."

"Indeed!" exclaimed she, "but I can see that you have travelled."

"I spent two years in England."

"As everything English is the rage just now, I dare say you recognize my dress."

The young stranger was forced to confess that he did not, and he avowed that he had attended but little to the affairs of the toilette during his absence; but his manner implied that he had now seen one that he should not readily forget. Well, to cut the conversation much shorter than the countess did, they parted, with a light hint just dropped by Amalie, that she now passed the greater portion of her time in solitude, and that the old chestnut was her favourite haunt. The next day she was there, and the young stranger passed quite accidentally; however, she had to show him how much more securely the paroquet was fastened to-day; one word led to another, and the conversation was long and interesting. Amalie discovered that the youth's name was Julian; and that he was démocrate en misanthrope, but she undertook to convert him. Even with the very prettiest of preceptors conversion is not the work of a day; so leaving it to its progress, we will take the opportunity of stating who Julian was—alas! a roturier. His father had carried on an extensive trade in precious stones, had travelled much, and profited in more ways than one by his travels; he early realised a competence, and, what is much rarer, early began to enjoy it. He married an English girl, and settling in the valley where he was born, led a life of seclusion, study, and domestic content—a state of existence so often a dream and so rarely a reality. Julian was brought up with every care; his natural talents were cultivated as sedulously as books could cultivate them. But the knowledge of the library is not that of the world; a youth of solitude is bad preparation for a manhood of action; from the earliest age we need to mingle with our kind; the child corrects and instructs the child more than their masters; our equals are the tools wherewith experience works out its lessons; and the play-ground, with its rival interests, its injustices, its necessity for the ready wit and the curbed temper is both miniature and prophesy of the world, which will but bring back the old struggles only with a sterner aspect, and the same successes, but with more than half their enjoyment departed.

The death of Julian's mother was soon followed by that of his father, and at nineteen the youth was left to a world from which he turned with all the desolation that attends on the first acquaintance with sorrow and death. The affection between himself and his parents had been so strong and undivided, that life seemed left without a charm when bereaved of their love. Youth suffers but for a season; the bowed but unbroken spirit resumes its elasticity; the future, unknown and beautiful, wins the present to itself, and the past waits for that dark and overwhelming influence which sooner or later will darken our whole horizon.

Julian arrived in Paris—his heart full of passion, and his head full of poetry—the one to be deceived, and the other to be disappointed. His wealth, his prepossessing appearance, and some scientific introductions, for his father had been the correspondent of eminent men, opened to him several of the first houses in Paris; but such society soon made him aware that he was only there on sufferance; that "thus far and no further," was the motto of aristocratic courtesy; he felt himself the equal—ay, the superior—of half the gracious coxcombs that surrounded him, and yet an accident of birth and fortune placed him at an immeasurably distance from those whose manner mocked him with the semblance of equality. It was one of the greatest vices of the old French regime, that there was no opening for the energy, the enthusiasm, or the genius, of the middle rank; that rank which in England is constantly renovating the upper classes, and which may, at least, aspire to any distinction. But in France, "the sword, gown, glory" did not "offer in exchange" for industry and talent; and a highly educated young man, of independent fortune, but of plebeian extraction,—from his wealth lacking the only pursuit allotted to his class—was like an animal in a menagerie, the most misplaced object in creation, debarred from all healthy and natural exercise, yet able to see the free boughs and far prospect while confined to a dreary perch and a narrow cage. But the tyranny of custom, like all other tyrannies, when grown quite unbearable—for it is wonderful what people will endure—had already sown the seeds of its own dissolution. Out of the hardship had grown the repining, and to repine at the exercise of an alleged right is soon to question its authority, and the first question asked shakes the whole ancient and time-honoured fabric of privilege. A fierce and restless spirit of change was at work—and only that the future, despite of history, was never yet foretold from the past, a sudden and terrible re-action might have been foreseen. But we have nothing more to do with revolutionary principles than to mark their effect on the mind of Julian, which soon became imbued with the wildest of the doctrines then afloat; to the young it seems so easy to mend everything, simply because they have not tried. Perfect equality, and perfect despotism, are theories equally unreducible to practice; but there are many fine sentiments belonging to the first, and there is singular fascination in a fine sentiment—we pay ourselves a compliment by uttering it. Julian heard the errors of "the present state of things" so often dilated upon, that he doubted whether there was anything really right on the earth; however, he was fortunate in the belief (a common patriotic delusion, by-the-by,) that himself, together with a few chosen others, were destined to set everything as it ought to be, and the sooner that such a destiny was fulfilled the better. In the meantime an affront at a gaming-table from the Chevalier de l'Escars, for which satisfaction was afterwards refused on the plea he could not fight a roturier, drove Julian's naturally violent temper almost to insanity. Degraded in his own eyes, he fancied every one must feel as he did, and abjured a world to which he imagined he was an object of scorn, while in truth he was only one of indifference. There is one conviction at which, though forced upon us by daily experience, we never arrive, namely, the conviction that Nobody in reality cares for Anybody; but this truth is so cold that we fence it out by all sorts of cloaks and coverings, delusions and devices. Well, Julian retired to his native valley, to brood over schemes of public benefit and private revenge; but at two-and-twenty it is as much trop tôt for a man to be philosophe as it is for a woman to be dévote. Les beaux yeux of Madame de Boufflers put to flight a thousand schemes for the regeneration of mankind, and Julian forgot wrongs, projects, equality, unity, and the rights of the human race, at the feet of the pretty aristocrat.

PART II

A low, chill wind moaned through the streets of Paris, and a dull, small rain scarcely penetrated the thick fog which hung on the oppressed atmosphere:—in a high wind and a brisk shower there is something that exhilarates the spirits; but this damp, dreary weather relaxes every nerve, unless indeed they be highly strung with some strong excitement, that defies every external influence—but, ah! of such life has but few instances. All great cities present strange contrasts; the infinite varieties of human existence gathered together mock each other with the wildest contrasts; and if this be true of all cities and all times, what must it have been in an hour like that of which we now write, and in a capital like Paris! The revolution was now raging in all its horrors; a terrible desire for blood had risen up in the minds of men, and cruelty had become as much a passion as love. In one street a band of ruffians insulted the quiet night with their frightful orgies; in the next a worn and devoted family clung to each other, and trembled lest the wind as it moaned past might bring the footsteps of the ministers of a nation's vengeance, or rather of a nation's madness. Here was a prison crowded with ghastly wretches sickening on hope deferred, till it grew into fear; there a palace where the purple availed no longer, while its wearied and wretched inmates sought courage from despair. Hate, terror, rage, revenge, all the most ghastly elements of human wretchedness and crime, were in commotion, and Paris was filled with riot and change. Yet into one luxurious haunt of rank, wealth, and grace it would seem as if no alteration had made its way. The blue satin draperies of the little boudoir, which was fitted up as a tent, were undisturbed, and the silver muslin curtains reflected back the soft light of the lamps; while roses, on which months of care had been bestowed for an hour of lavish bloom, the red light from the cheerful hearth, the rich carpet, over which the step passed noiseless, the perfumes that exhaled their fragrant essence—all mocked the desolation without. Leaning upon a couch near the window was the Comtesse

Amalie, pretty as ever, changed in nothing save costume, which was suited to the classical mania of the day; her hair was gathered up in a Grecian knot, the little foot wore a sandal, and the white robe, à l'antique, was fastened by cameos. Suddenly a door opened—and the rain damp upon his cloak, and his hair glittering with its moisture, entered Julian; he was changed, for he looked pale and exhausted, and lip and brow wore the fixed character and the deeper line which passion ever leaves behind. Amalie rose, and, with an expression of the tenderest welcome, took his cloak from him, and with her own mignon hands drew the fauteuil towards the fire, and then placing herself on a little stool at his feet, looked up in his face with an asking and anxious gaze, perhaps the most touching that a woman's features can assume to her lover. Amalie did not love Julian as he loved her—it was not in her nature—but her light and vain temper was subdued by his earnest and impetuous one; she feared him too, and fear is the great strengthener of a woman's love. Besides there is something in intense passion that communicates itself, as the warmth of the sun colours the cloud, whose frail substance is yet incapable of retaining the light or heat. Amalie had no sympathy with the poetry of his character; but it gave grace to his flattery and variety to himself, to say nothing of the advantage of contrast with all her other adorateurs. Moreover his influence with the Jacobin clubs had warded off dangers that had crushed other families as noble as that of De Boufflers. Julian, like all of an imaginative turn, deceived himself, and worshipped an idol which he had created rather than an object which existed: a pretty face blinds even a philosopher, and from habits of seclusion and naturally refined taste, he was peculiarly susceptible to the charm and ease of her manners. Perhaps—for the wheat and tares of human motives spring up inextricably blended—the young democrat was somewhat dazzled by the rank of the charming countess. I always suspect that the professed despisers of all worldly distinctions take refuge in disdain from desire. For some time Julian sat in moody silence, his gaze fixed on the wood embers, as if absorbed in contemplating their fantastic combinations. Amalie changed her attitude, rallied her lover on his abstraction, and asked him if it was fair to seek one lady's presence and then think of another.

"Think of another!" exclaimed he, springing from his seat: "Good God, Amalie! is there one moment, fevered and hurried as is my existence, in which you are forgotten? I love you terribly! ay, terribly! for it is terrible to have one's very soul so bound up in but one object. I would rather at this very moment see you dead at my feet than even dream of you as loving another."

The countess turned pale; there was nothing in herself that responded to this burst of passion, and terror was her paramount sensation. "You are too violent," said she, in a faltering voice.

"Too sincere, you mean," replied he. "Amalie, our present life is intolerable; I cannot endure longer these stolen and brief interviews. Why should we thus waste life's short season of existence? we shall not live long,—let us live together. Amalie, you must fly with me." Madame de Boufflers looked—what she was—astounded at this proposition. "What nonsense you are talking to-night," answered she, forcing a laugh.

"You do not love me!" and his clear light eyes flashed upon her with a strange mixture of ferocity and tenderness.

She shrank before the glance, and whispered, "If I did not love you, why are you here? but think of the scandal of an elopement; les convenances of society must be respected."

"Curse on these social laws! which are made for the convenience of the few and the degradation of the many. Amalie, I cannot, will not steal into the house of that insolent aristocrat, your husband, like a midnight thief. You must leave him, and let my home become yours. I will watch over you,—pass my life at your side,—anticipate your slightest wish,—but you must be mine own. The law for divorce will soon pass the Assembly, and then let me add what tie or form you will to the deep devotion of my heart, my own, my beloved Amalie, as my wife."

"Your wife!" interrupted the countess, old prejudices springing up far stronger than present feelings. "How very absurd; think for a moment of the difference in our rank."

A spasm of convulsive emotion passed over his face, the veins rose on the high forehead, the blood started from the bitten lip, but in an instant the expression was subdued into a stern coldness; and if Julian's voice was somewhat hoarse the words were slow and distinct. "Amalie," said he, taking her hands in his, "my whole destiny turns on the result of this interview. Have you no fear of my despair?"

Amalie could have answered that she felt very sufficiently afraid at that moment, but, for once in her life she was at a loss for a reply; she remained silent, almost embarrassed, certainly bored,—and Julian went on.

"I will not shock your gentle ear by words of hate against the class to which you belong; but a fearful reckoning is at hand; and I am among those who will exact it to the uttermost. I warn you fly from them—be mine, for your own sake."

"Really, Monsieur Julian," said she, "your conduct tonight is most unaccountable. Come, do pray be a little more amusing."

"Monsieur Julian!" repeated he, in a deep whisper; "is it come to this? Amalie, do, I implore you, think how desperately I love you. You may believe that on your part it has been the sacrifice; but what has it been on mine? For your sake I have trifled with rights I hold most sacred; I have tampered with mine own integrity; I have held back from the great task before me; I have been a faint and slow follower of that glorious freedom which now calls aloud on all her worshippers for the most entire devotion; and yet I have shrank back from the appointed duty. Amalie, come with me—be my inspiration; feel as I feel, think as I think, cast aside the idle prejudices of a selfish and profligate court, and be repaid by passion as fervent, as fond, and as faithful as ever beat in man's heart for the woman of his first and only love."

"This is really too much of a good thing," thought the countess, whose mind wandered from the love before her to the scandal and ridicule likely to be caused by her flight. "Il faut respecter les convenances," was her chilling reply.

Julian dropped her hands, and approached the door; he opened it, but he lingered on the threshold. "Do you let me go, Amalie?" whispered he, in a scarcely audible voice.

"I am sure," replied Madame de Boufflers, pettishly, "you have not been so agreeable that I should wish to detain you."

The door closed, and his rapid steps were heard descending the narrow staircase; at length they died away.

"I really must put an end to this affair, it is becoming troublesome; my young republican is growing pedante et despote. He has none of the graces of my cousin Eugene." And Madame de Boufflers threw herself into the fauteuil, and indulged in a discontented reverie, in which Julian's faults and Eugene's merits occupied conspicuous places; together with the garniture of a new species of sandal which she meditated producing. In the meantime Julian pursued his way through the dark and dreary streets, suffering that agony of disappointed affection which the heart can know but once. Love is very blind indeed, but let the veil once be removed, though but for a moment, and it never can be replaced again. Then how quick-sighted do we become to the errors of our past worship, and mortification adds bitterness to regret. "And is it for one," exclaimed he, "who holds the factitious advantage of a name, to be better worth than my deep love, that I have sacrificed the cause to which I was vowed, and have paused on the noblest path to which man ever devoted his energies? But the weakness is over; a terrible bond shall be made with Liberty—Liberty henceforth my only hope, my only mistress!"

The evil spirit of love left his soul for a moment, but returned, though with a strange and lurid aspect, bringing with him other and worse spirits than himself—hate, revenge, blood-thirstiness—all merged in and coloured by the excited and fanatic temper of the time. He stopped before a large hotel, from whose windows the red light glared, as if it mocked the darkness of night as much as the revel within did its silence. There was that mixture of luxury and disorder which at once so shocks and attracts the imagination. Its hangings were silk, the chairs and sofas satin, but they were torn and soiled; the servants were many, but ill-dressed and awkward; all the light elegance for which the hotel had been noted in its former proprietor's life (the Duc de N. had perished by the guillotine) had disappeared; the character of its present master was impressed on all around him. A door opened into a vast chamber crowded with fierce and eager faces, every eye assuming the expression of murder as the ruthless Danton called down their vengeance on those whom he denominated their old and arrogant oppressors.

"Some there are," exclaimed he, as he caught sight of Julian's pale and expressive countenance, "who delude themselves with the belief that their own preferences are sufficient cause for exception—who merge the public cause in private interests. What are such but cowards and traitors? unworthy to bring one stone towards the great temple of liberty about to overshadow the world, but whose foundations must be laid in blood—ay, blood!"

A hoarse and sullen murmur rather than acclamation ran through the crowd, and a few minutes elapsed ere the business of the night proceeded. Then began those fearful denunciations, which seemed to loosen every tie of nature—the father witnessed against the son, and the son against the father; the young, the aged, the innocent, the beautiful, were alike marked as victims. Suddenly Julian arose: a close observer might have noted that his brow was knit, as it is in inward pain, that his lip was white, as if the life-current had been driven back upon the heart, prophetic of the future, which doomed it to freeze there for ever; but to the careless eye he seemed stern, calm, ferocious as the rest, while he denounced Amalie, Comtesse de Boufflers, as an aristocrat, and an enemy to the people. Danton looked at him for an instant, but cowered before the wild and fiery glance that met his own.

To denounce, to condemn, to execute, were, in those ruthless days, but the work of four-and-twenty hours. The next noon but one an almost insensible female form was carried or rather dragged to the scaffold. It was the Comtesse Amalie. Her long bright hair fell in disorder over her shoulders; the executioner gathered it up in a rough knot,—he had been told not to sever it from the graceful head. At that moment the prisoner gave a bewildered stare around—a wild gleam of hope illumined her features—she stretched out her arms to some one passionately in the crowd. "Julian, save me!" The executioner forced her to her knee—the axe glittered in the sun, and the head fell into the appointed basket, while a convulsive motion shook the white garments around the quivering trunk.

PART III

"I looked on the faces of his judges, and felt there was no hope," said an old man as he led away the promised bride of his son, now a prisoner, doomed to death on the morrow.

"Yet the one they call Julian looks so young, so pale, and so sad, there is surely some touch of pity in him; at least, I will kneel at his feet, and implore him for mercy on Frederic."

The old man shook his head, but accompanied her to Julian's hotel, where the eloquence of some golden coins procured her admittance. She found her way to a large and gloomy chamber, where he sat surrounded with books, papers, and charts, mocking himself with a frenzied belief in the coming amelioration of the world, while his own home was a desert and his own heart a desolation. He did not perceive the fair and agitated creature that knelt at his feet, till her supplicating and broken voice roused his attention. He listened till her words died away into the short thick sobs of utter agony, unable to bear the picture it had conjured up of its coming wretchedness.

"Pity from me!" he exclaimed, with a quick fierce laugh; "Pity!—I do not know the meaning of the word. You might as well address your prayers to yonder bust of the stern old Roman, who sealed his country's freedom with the life-blood of his child."

The girl unconsciously looked towards the harsh features, made yet harsher by the dark marble in which they were carved. And she started, for she felt that even that stern and sculptured countenance had more of human sympathy than the pale lip and cold eye of the living listener; yet love is desperate in its hope; she flung herself at his feet, she hid her face on the hand which she grasped, for she dared not look up and meet that fixed and passionless face; but still she pleaded as those plead who pray for a life far dearer than their own.

"He is so young—so good—there is so much happiness before us; his poor old father will die—he has no other child—and I—-he must not look to me to supply his place. God of heaven! have you never loved—have you no recollections of affection that can move you to pity others!"

"I have!" said Julian; and rising from his seat, he took the arm of the agitated girl, and led her to a recess in the apartment, and drew back a curtain. Horror for a moment suspended every other feeling; for, laid upon a cushion, the long fair hair streaming around, was a female head, preserved by some curious chemical process; the eyes were closed, but as if in sleep; colour had departed from lip and cheek, and something beyond even the rigidity of stone was on the face. The petitioner turned from the dead to the living, whose ashy colour, and wild fierce eye, struck more terror to her soul than the mournful mockery of the head, where life's likeness was fearfully rendered. Julian gazed on the dread memorial which he had snatched from the scaffold, with that strange mixture of hate and love, the mind's most terrible element, whereof comes despair and madness; then turning slowly to the bewildered girl, said, in a low voice, but whose whisper was like thunder when the flash is commissioned to destroy,—

"That head belonged to my mistress—she was an aristocrat—and I denounced her—Judge if there exist one human being whom my pity is likely to spare."

His wretched petitioner gazed upwards, but hopelessly, and staggered against the wall.

"I would be alone," said Julian, and led her to the door.

She left him silently. She now knew prayers were vain, That night her lover perished beneath the guillotine;—the same blow struck to the heart of the fond faithful girl—death was merciful, for both died at the same moment. By some inscrutable sympathy with love which yet moved him not to spare, Julian had them buried in the same grave.

THE LOVE CHARM

"Very well, indeed. I see that I shall make quite a gardener of you in time." The fair girl to whom this was addressed looked up in the old man's face with a smile, and then went on with her task. This task consisted in tying up various flowering annuals, which, like many other things in this world, required a little wholesome restraint. A pretty little garden it was on which they were, bestowing so much pains, both useful and ornamental. The straight green rows of beans had some tall stalks among them, that might have emulated their classical ancestor, on which Jack the Giant Killer mounted to the Ogre's castle, and the peas deserved all the praises which it did their master's heart good to hear lavished upon them. There was a background of cabbages, and some artichokes overlooked the neat quickset hedge. Gooseberries and currants were beginning to redden amid their verdant leaves, the cherries were looking a sort of yellow coral, and the small crisp apples were already set. A blue tint was already appearing on the lavender, and the pale young shoots were springing in the box edges which neatly surrounded the small flower-bed. The porch at the door was covered with China roses, pretty delicate frail things without scent. But this was compensated by the cabbage roses, now opening their crimson depths full of summer and sweetness, wearing the richest blush that ever welcomed June.

Adam Leslie was a happy man—he had all that a long life had desired—a window looking into a street—his house was the last of a row, a garden, and a small competence. He had past a number of years in the very heart of the city, where a dusty geranium, a pot of mignonette, and a blackbird, were all he had to remind him of his boyhood and his native Argyleshire. He kept a small shop, whose profits just, and only just, maintained a wife and a large family. They were not destined long to be the burthen which in his moments of temper he sometimes called them,—wife, children, were carried one after another to the crowded church-yard in the next street. He wished that they had been buried in the country, for the country to him was the ideal of existence. Years past away, and found him still the same hard-working man, toiling he scarcely knew for what. Suddenly a new tie again bound him to existence. His brother died, and left an orphan daughter to his charge. Once more that dark and narrow staircase was musical with childish feet—and Adam Leslie no longer sat down to an unshared and silent board. The timid quiet little stranger soon became to him even as a child of his own. She had the blue eyes and bright hair of those that he had lost. Like them she soon became anxious for her. The cheek grew paler day by day; the little feet lost their lightness; and the languid lip poured forth less and less frequent its snatches of mountain song. Marion was accustomed to air and exercise, and pined in the close street. "Can I not keep even one to be the joy of my old age," thought the old man as he looked on the pale and spiritless child, who had drawn her stool towards him, and was resting her head on his knee. His resolution was taken—he gave up sundry visions of wealth and civic honours that of late had troubled him overmuch—and gathering together what he had, gave up the pursuit of more. He sold his shop, and retired, as we have before said, on a small but comfortable independence. He took a small house at Greenwich—something of lingering habit still kept him near to the great city where he had passed so many years, and at first, it must be confessed, he found time rather heavy on his hands. But an active mind soon makes occupation for itself, and in the course of a year Leslie had quite enough to do. In the meantime he was amply rewarded by the improvement in Marion. The change did wonders for her. The cheek recovered its blooming colour, and amended health soon showed itself in the amended spirits. Often and often, when at work in his garden, he heard her sweet laugh, like musical bells in the distance; and her soft voice singing those old songs which yet struck a chord in his heart.

But Marion, from the rosy child, was now grown up into the lovely young woman, and there was one in particular who thought her so. Her engagement with Edward Meredith was known to, and approved by her uncle—certainly, in the first instance, he did say that Marion might have done better—yet, a little eloquence on the part of the lover, and a little silence and a few blushes on the part of the mistress, obtained his consent.

Young Meredith had his way to make in the world, but his steadiness and activity had made him a favourite with the merchant in whose counting-house he was a clerk, and, in a couple more years, he confidently calculated on being able to support a wife. Adam Leslie had not much to give during his life, but at his death Marion would inherit his little property. In this they were as happy as youth and hope could make. Expectation is in itself a very pretty sort of reality. Night after night Edward used to row, or if the wind served, sail down the Thames, and land about a mile above Greenwich, when a quarter of an hour's rapid walking brought him to Leslie's house. He usually arrived there about eight, which just left time for a walk in the fine old park with Marion. Slowly did they wander through those green and shadowy glades, where the deer feed so fearlessly, conscious, though scarce observant, of the beauty around them. They had no eyes for the Venetian palace at their side, through whose divided domes are seen the masts of a thousand ships. They looked not on the mighty city dark in the distance, nor on the green country that stretched far away; they had eyes only for each other. But the natural influences around were not unfelt, the soft air aided her companion's words to raise the rich colour on Marion's cheek; and Edward grew more eloquent with the free breath that he drew on the fresh and open height, which the Scotch girl laughed at him for calling hills. At nine punctually they returned to the house, when Marion used to disappear for a few minutes, "on hospitable cares intent," and she and supper came in together. They say suppers are very unwholesome, our grandfathers and grandmothers never discovered it, and Adam Leslie belonged to them; at all events, it was very pleasant, when on a summer evening the little table was drawn to the window seat, which two of the party found quite large enough for their accommodation, and on the other side the old man in his large arm-chair. In this seat Adam Leslie had three sources of happiness, he saw his supper, the clematis he had planted and trained round the window, and the young people who were to him as his children. "We shall have a thunder-shower soon," had been his prophecy the whole day,—"The wish had been father to the thought;"—still hour after hour the dark clouds had passed provokingly away, taking their showers with them; however, they were now gathering in good earnest. A low clap of thunder growled in the distance, and the wind awoke on the branches. A shower of leaves, green fresh leaves falling before their time, whirled through the air. This was followed by the pelting rain, and Edward shut down the window. The gardener congratulated himself and his peas and beans, and the supper went on with added cheerfulness. Suddenly Edward exclaimed, "Look, Marion, how beautiful!" She turned and saw the clear silvery crescent of the new moon just emerged from a black cloud; a ring of blue sky was around, and the edges of the dense vapour were touched with light.

"Ah!" exclaimed Marion, who had all the ready superstition of a mountaineer, "I have seen the new moon through glass for the first time, and you, Edward, have shown it me."

"It is very unlucky," continued her uncle, "to see the new moon through glass for the first time."

Edward tried to laugh at the superstition, but unshared mirth only damps the spirits of a small circle, and he gave up the attempt. That night they parted somewhat sooner and less cheerfully than usual. The next morning was too glad and sunny for any ill omen to be recollected, and by a sort of tacit agreement the moon was kept quite out of the conversation, Marion a little ashamed of a belief which she could not reason upon, and Edward as little liking to renew any subject in which he could not agree with her.

A fortnight passed away, and the moon was at its full; Edward was now later of an evening than he usually had been, for an extreme pressure of business on the house in which he was employed made the work of extra hours necessary, and he was only too glad to do anything that put him forward in his master's favour. One night he was returning very late, but the tide served, the night was a lovely night in June, and he enjoyed it, as those enjoy whose naturally poetic temperament is checked by their ordinary circumstances, but which lends the keenest delight to any touch of romance or beauty that breaks in upon the commonplace. He floated down the noble river with a navy resting on its dark stream. The light arched bridges, with the long lines of light trembling through them, were left far behind. The huge dome of St. Paul's arose bathed in the moonlight, that giant fane of a giant city, a hundred spires were shining silvery in the soft gleam, and all meaner objects were touched with a picturesque obscurity: all around was silence and rest. The myriad voices of London were still, and nothing vexed the lulled ear of midnight. The only sounds were those that might have soothed even the ear of sleep—there was the languid waving to and fro of some loose sail, and the dip of Edward's oars. His little boat was the only moving thing on the water, for if the black colliers, whose gloomy canvass was still spread, moved, the movement was imperceptible. But his light boat went on and left behind a train of glittering bubbles, like the small stars that meet and mingle on the milky way.

He had now arrived at that more lonely portion of the river which preceded his landing. A little tired with rowing, he let the oars drop, and his boat glided with the stream, as he leant back gazing on the clear heaven above. He started, for a wild strain of music floated on the ear. It was interrupted for a moment by the chiming of the clocks that, one mingling with another, told the hour of twelve. They ceased, and the music rose distinct upon the ear. He gazed around and saw, far away in the moonlight, a little boat, with a white and swelling sail. He rowed towards it, and could distinguish the chords of some lute-like instrument, and the tones of a human voice. As he came nearer, he saw that the little bark lay motionless on the river, and that it only held one person. The figure was too much muffled for observation, but the flowing drapery denoted a woman—even if the sweet voice had left it doubtful— Edward remained entranced by the delicious singing. The air was singularly wild, and the words were in a foreign tongue, but he thought in his heart he had never listened to music before. After pausing while

"His spirit like a swan did float
Upon the silver breath of that sweet singing,"

he rowed eagerly towards the mysterious bark. A dense cloud sailed over the moon, and the river for a few moments was shrouded in complete darkness. The moonlight softly broke through the dusky barrier, the dense veil melted into soft and glittering vapour; again the river was flooded with light, but the music had ceased, and the boat was gone. Edward strained his eyes in gazing round the horizon, but in vain.—He listened, but no sound broke the profound stillness till the clocks struck one. He started from the reverie in which he had been indulging, and snatching up the oars, rowed hastily to the landing-place. Fastening his boat, he proceeded hastily along the lane which he had so often trodden. Twice he paused to breathe the cool fresh air, for he was feverish, and his temples were throbbing, while that sweet strange air would not quit his ear. Late as it was, there was a light in the window of Adam Leslie's cottage, and a light step stole along the passage, and a soft hand unbarred the door; a few whispered words were all on which they might venture, for her uncle would have been miserable at the idea of Marion keeping such late vigils. Edward's sleep that night was broken and troubled—that song haunted him. In his dreams he was again upon the water, he drew near to the strange boat, he spoke to its lady, and she raised her veil, and he gazed on a face beautiful beyond all that he had dreamed of beauty. Morning came at last, but he woke weary and fevered.

"How ill you look, dearest Edward," said Marion, when they met at their early breakfast, "you are overworking yourself;" and she gazed upon him with a tender anxiety which left him not a thought but for herself. She walked with him down to the boat, yet he never alluded to the mysterious music of the preceding night, though it still rang in his ear, and mingled with even her sweet voice; a shyness for which he could not himself account prevented his alluding to the subject, he shrank from naming it; and when he reached the river, he cast a hasty and confused glance around, as if it must retain some consciousness. But all was bustle and life, the ships taking advantage of a favourable wind, were under a press of canvass, and boat and barge were in full activity. Children were playing on the banks, and their shrill voices and laughter softened the deeper tones of manhood and business. Edward sought in vain that day to fix his attention to the desk before him; still he heard that sweet low song, and faces of strange loveliness floated before him. He was impatient for night, and when it came, he sprung into his boat, half fearfully, half eagerly. It was as his heart foreboded, again he heard that melancholy song— again he saw the veiled figure in the little boat—the clocks too told the same hour, but this time he rowed at once towards the stranger's bark. The lady flung back her veil, and he at once recognised the lovely face that had so haunted his dreams. She stretched forth her hand, as their boats lay alongside, and he took the small white fingers, that glittered in the moonlight with gems, in his own. But the touch was as an electric shock, his boat seemed to sink from under him, a mighty sound was in his ears, and he sank back insensible.

He awoke as from sleep, confused and dizzy: he gazed round, and as he gradually recovered his senses, saw that he was in a vast hall. He lay for a while in a pleasant state of half consciousness, his gaze slowly taking note of the various objects by which he was surrounded. The hall was surrounded by pillars of malachite, wrought into the semblance of gigantic serpents that supported the shining dome, and whose illumined heads made an enormous lamp in the centre. The partitions they formed were filled either by alcoves crowded with birds of rich and foreign plumage, or by paintings representing scenes in some far country. At one end was a large fountain which played in fantastic forms round an inner basin that shone with liquid fire, and mingled its reddening jets with the fountain's clear and crystal ones. At the other end was a conservatory, crowded with large beautiful flowers, but none of them familiar to Edward. Marble urns scattered around were wreathed with their magnificent blossoms, and some of the birds, loosened from the golden network, flitted past; some with crests of meteor-like crimson, others spreading vast and radiant pinions coloured from the sunset. The waving of their pinions, and the falling of the fountain, were the only sounds heard in that stately hall;—these, and one other: it was the low soft breathing of a woman. Edward heard it, and turning to the side from whence it came, saw, watching by his side, the strange beauty of the song and of the boat. She was tall beyond the ordinary height of woman, but stately in her grace as the ideal of a queen and the reality of a swan. Her arms and feet were bare, but for the gems which encircled them. A white robe swept around her in folds gathered at the waist by a golden girdle inscribed with signs and characters. Her hair was singularly thick, and of that purple blackness seen on the grape and the neck of the raven—black, with a sort of azure bloom upon it. It was fastened in large folds, which went several times round the head, and these were adorned with jewels and precious stones, like a midnight lighted with stars. Her complexion was a pale pure olive, perfectly colourless, but delicate as that of a child. Her mouth was the only spot where the rose held dominion, and lips of richer crimson never opened to the morning.

"Youth," said she, in a low voice of peculiar sweetness, "I love thee;—night after night I have watched thy boat on yonder river. I know not what the customs of thy land may be;—I speak according unto mine. I have wealth—I have power—I have knowledge;—I can share them all with thee." Edward started to his feet—the image of Marion was uppermost in his thoughts. "Lady," he replied, unconsciously imitating her own high-wrought language, "in my country woman pleads not to man. I have not wooed, and I do not wish to win thee. Thou art wonderful and very fair, but thou art not my love."

She looked at him for a moment with her large dark eyes. "I think," continued she, "I could make thee love me, if thou wert to stay here awhile. I pray thee, give me a lock of your sunny hair. I have seen none like it."

Edward gave her one of the bright curls which clustered golden around his head.

"Look around thee," said the lady, "for a little time. This hall is a triumph of my art. These birds and flowers belong to my native Mexico, and so do those glad valleys."

Edward gazed around in wonder, and while he gazed there came on the air the same melancholy song that he had heard while on the river. The very sound of his own steps disturbed him; and he flung himself on a couch, to enjoy without interruption the exquisite melody. The intense perfume of the flowers intoxicated him like wine. He felt as if lulled in a delicious trance, in which one image became more and more distinct—the pale but lovely face of his hostess. His heart was filling with love for those radiant eyes. A softer fragrance breathed around him—it was her breath. He looked, and she was again bending over him; he saw himself mirrored in the moonlight of her eyes.

"You will not leave me?" whispered she, in those soft sweet tones which were like notes from a lute.

"Never!" exclaimed the youth, and threw himself at her feet.

Weeks had passed away, and done the work of years in Adam Leslie's cottage. His garden was now in the richest season of the year. The sunshine had settled into crimson on the peach; the bloom was on the plum, and the dahlias, whose colours might vie with a monarch's clothing, crowded the garden with unwonted prodigality. Arm-in-arm the old man and his niece wandered around the now mournful garden; he trying to speak that comfort which his every look belied, and she trying to smile as if she believed him; but the tears rose into her eyes as she tried to smile. It was now more than six weeks since Edward's mysterious disappearance, and the little hope that had once been cherished was now dying fast away. That night, after Adam Leslie had gone to bed, Marion strolled into the garden. She could not sleep, and the lovely moonlight she thought might soothe her. Alas, the tears that had been in her eyes all day now began to flow, when suddenly the sound of footsteps roused her attention. She raised her face from her hands, and saw a little deformed negro-woman standing beside her.

"Why do you cry," said the strange visitor, fixing on her a pair of small, bright, snake-like eyes, "like a child, when you might win your lover back like a woman?"

Marion stood silent with extreme astonishment, and the woman went on. "Yes, if you will follow me—though you look as if you were frightened to death, I can help you to set your lover free. There are other bright eyes in the world besides your own; but yours will be the best and last loved, if you dare to follow one who is your friend." "I will ask my uncle," said Marion, trembling with agitation.

"You must ask no one, and nothing"—interrupted the little negro, her harsh voice growing yet harsher as she raised it—"but your own true heart: unless there be love enough to lead you on, your lover will remain bound by the spells of the sorceress for ever."

The thought past rapidly through Marion's mind, that if she could but see Edward, old love must revive, even if he had deserted her for another. Led on by some strange fascination, she followed the little negro woman. They came to the river side, where a small boat was moored, and when her companion was seated, took up the oars and began rowing with great quickness down the river. They stopped at a small flight of wooden steps, and an almost worn-out door admitted them into a large, but desolate-looking garden; another door, but that huge and massy, admitted them into a dark and winding passage. Marion shuddered as the little negro caught her hand to lead her forward; she followed her for some distance, when the sudden opening of another door dazzled her eyes with a blaze of light. They had entered a magnificent chamber, fitted up in the utmost oriental luxury for a sleeping-room. Marion was scarcely allowed time to look around, for her dwarfish companion whispered in a low tone, like the hissing of a serpent, "Open that gold box, and take out the lock of hair you see there; it is your lover's." Well did the forsaken girl recollect the sunny hair; she pressed it to her lips, while her fast-falling tears dimmed its lustre.

"Come, come, I will show him to you," exclaimed the little negro woman, again hurrying her on; "if you still love him, when you see him, throw that charmed lock of hair into the fountain of fire by which we shall be standing, and the spell that binds him will be broken."

Marion had not power to speak, but she followed the dwarfish creature with a heart beating louder than her steps. Again her eyes closed in the presence of sudden splendour, they were standing behind the fountain of mingled fire and water; from thence they could see without being seen. In the centre of that gorgeous hall, a lady was seated on a mattress covered with cloth of gold, and Edward was at her feet. They had eyes but for each other, and her one hand was in his, while the other was twisted in his bright hair.

"Now girl," hissed the same whisper, "fling the lock you hold in the fire."

Marion almost mechanically obeyed; she flung it, and a burst of thunder shook the building—the little fountain grew crimson, as if with blood; but one heart-piercing shriek rang above every other sound—it came from the dark lady.

"Hast thou found me, oh my enemy?" said she in the same low, sweet voice; but which now seemed the very echo of a broken heart.

"Aye," cried the little negro woman, "the dark spell has the mastery."

At this moment Marion rushed forward; she had seen Edward sink back convulsed on the couch—she threw herself on her knees beside, and supported his head—the dews of death were upon it. The tall and stately lady stood by, paler than marble, and even her bright lips colour less. Still her radiant eyes flashed defiance on the negro dwarf; but the heart's agony was in the compressed mouth, and with tears in those starry eyes, she turned to Edward. Marion saw her approach, and clasping him passionately in her arms, exclaimed—

"He is mine, loved long before you knew him—let us at least die together."

"Ah," exclaimed the stranger, "is it even so; I knew not of it."

A shrill wild laugh came from the little negro woman, and a faint cry from Marion; for Edward had sank down exhausted from her arm. Once more he unclosed his eyes, and fixing them on Marion with a look full of tenderness, murmured her name, and expired. The dark lady leant over him for a moment; whatever might be the anguish of that moment, she subdued it; but the veins swelled like chords in her clear temples, with the effort. She turned, and gave one look at the negro, who crouched beneath it like a beaten hound, and remained as if rooted to the spot.

"Take him to your home," said she to Marion; "what I must do, your eyes would shrink to witness. I will offer you nothing; my love and my gifts turn to curses."

She stamped on the ground, and four strange figures came forward, and raising Marion and Edward, carried them into the boat by the stairs, and there left them. The wind and tide slowly drifted them along, and the maiden sat floating over the river, with her lover's head upon her knee. Once, and once only she raised her eyes. A wild, melancholy song came upon her ear, and a dark bark, dimly seen amid the grey vapours of morning, flitted past. On the deck she fancied she saw a tall figure with long floating hair, stand wringing her hands in some passionate despair. It past rapidly out of sight, and as it past, the melancholy song died away in the distance; never since has it been heard on the Thames. The boat that bore the living and the dead was met by some watermen, who conveyed them on shore. Marion was perfectly insensible, and was carried home in a brain fever, from which she never recovered. At the last gasp they thought her sensible, for her eyes wandered round the room in search of her uncle; she caught sight of his face—a scarcely perceptible smile past over her countenance, and in that smile she died. The house and garden still remain, but they have a lonely and mournful look. The old man plants no more flowers in his garden; the few that he watches grow in the churchyard. He has planted some rose bushes on the grave of the lovers; those he still tends and waters. They are the last link between this living world and himself. Night and morning he visits those tombs; but he never visits them without a prayer that the time may soon come when he shall sleep at their side.

THE CRUISE

"The small things of life are the terrible," says a popular writer of our day, and the saying is true. Let us all look back on the most important events of our life, and in what slight accidents have they originated! The following story seems to be but a succession of unlucky chances, and yet each was a link in the dark chain of human destiny.

Its scene lies in one of the gayest sea towns of Devonshire; one of those bathing places which, for about three months in every year, is astonished at its own gaiety, and when the season is over is obliged to be content with its own society, and its own natural loveliness. Gaiety in a place of this kind, is a different sort of gaiety to that in London. It is more familiar—more a thing of fits and snatches—belongs to the open air—and has a touch of wildness from the greenwood tree. No one more enjoyed the brief dissipation of her native town than Edith Trevanion. The heiress and beauty of the neighbourhood, the darling of her father (mother she had none), the delight of her circle, human life seemed to have made an exception in her favour. The troubles that vex the most prosperous existed not for her. Poverty she only knew by the pleasure of relieving it. Sickness and death had left her house at too early a period for her remembrance, for her mother died when she was a child in arms. Within the last few months a still deeper happiness had girdled her around. She was engaged to a young man, of family and fortune equal to her own; and, moreover, Arthur Ralegh was a very handsome young man. However, wherever there is any love in the case, there is never any want of a few miseries as well. Arthur was of a jealous temper, and this is a sore temptation to a petted beauty. Edith knew her power, and did not dislike using it. Truly and entirely attached herself—loving, too, with all the gay confidence of unbroken spirits and first affection—she could not enter into, and therefore could not allow for all the tender anxieties of her lover; she excused a little feminine teasing to herself, as a wholesome sort of moral discipline. It was an absolute duty to cure him of such a fault as jealousy. What would he be when once she was fairly married to him? In the meantime, the War-office combined with fate against the unfortunate lover—a regiment was suddenly quartered in the town. This was really too much. Poor Arthur was haunted by red coats. They lounged through the streets, they rode through shady lanes, they danced in the assembly rooms, they lunched here and they dined there; and when at last night arrived, it was "dreams and not sleep that came into his head." His visions were all of "the scarlet colour." No young lady's head in all the place could run more upon "the officers" than his own. Both the Majors were married—that was something to be thankful for; but the Colonel was single, and younger, and better looking than the generality of Colonels; and the junior officers were an unusually fine set of men—at least so they seemed to Arthur Ralegh. During the first month of their stay, he took them all in their turns. One day it was the fascinating Captain—the next it was the handsome Lieutenant; till it even reached the interesting Ensign.

At last, these flying fears settled into a good earnest fit, which had Captain Delaford for its object. The whole regiment was considered charming enough; but Captain Delaford was the most charming of all. We Londoners know nothing of hearts carried by beat of drum. "The officers" conveys no meaning to our ear. We have an idea that the guards are very gentle manlike, but the military go for nothing in the great system of London dissipation. A young lady, even in Knightsbridge, would stare to be asked "If the barracks did not make the neighbourhood very gay?" It would be something like the fair damsel at St Helena asking "if England was not exceedingly dull after the fleet sailed?" But in a country town a regiment is a very grand affair indeed! Parties are made for and by the officers; they light up a ball, and the young ladies feel that it is an opportunity for attachments happy and unhappy; and, as Mr Bennet in 'Pride and Prejudice' justly observed, "next to being engaged, it is something to be crossed in love." Edith Trevanion liked the increased gaiety, she liked too the admiration and the attention. But her heart was irrevocably gone, and the very thought of change never came into her head. But the more she was conscious of her own attachment, the less could she bear to have it made a perpetual subject of doubt. It was one very hot morning—for the summer had been unusually warm and long—that they were standing on a terrace which ran on the shady side of the house. They were walking up and down a little to Arthur's discontent, for he had been asking her to ride, which Edith refused on account of the extreme heat. She was herself in such gay spirits. Her father had just surprised her, and such surprises are very agreeable, by a set of turquoises, and she was convinced herself, and wanted to convince everybody else, that blue was the loveliest colour in the world. "It is the colour of the sky, of violets,"— "and," interrupted Arthur, "as Captain Delaford would say, of your eyes. I am sure that is just one of his pretty speeches." "Not quite," replied Edith; "you have a scowl where he has a smile—and you ought to put on an irresistible air while speaking." "An irresistible air" exclaimed Arthur. "So you think him irresistible" "At least our whole town does, and you would not have me opposed to general opinion. You know what an enemy you are to singularity in our sex." Arthur made no answer, but amused himself with picking off the heads of divers unoffending flowers. Edith began a curious examination of a bunch of Provence roses, which she held in her hand. Her own sweet mouth, with the smile dimpling round it, was like one of the buds, when the soft red first breaks through the green envelope. "But, at least," said Arthur, "you will not dance with Captain Delaford. I make a point of your not doing it." Now Ralegh was very wrong to make a point of any such trifle. It set the whole spirit of feminine insubordination up in arms. Besides, this very jealousy was an angry subject with Edith. She felt herself unworthily judged—and, moreover, her taste called in question. The very idea that she could think of such a man for one moment—she who quite piqued herself on having such an ideal standard of perfection—it was such a bad compliment. Captain Delaford all smiles, sighs, and douceurs to every lady he came near; he who cut out all his conversation by a pattern—well, it was too provoking! Had Arthur chosen to be jealous of the Colonel, who was pale and silent—therefore set down as having had an unhappy passion, and "so interesting;"— or even the young ensign, who was such a sweet poet, and had written some exquisite verses in her album, about moonlight, and blighted affection—either of these would have been some credit. But Captain Delaford—the singing, flirting, universal Captain Delaford—it was really too bad! "Not dance with him!" exclaimed she, with the prettiest air of surprise in the world. "Why, I would sooner dance with him than any one else—he is the best waltzer in the room." "And I am the worst" interrupted Arthur angrily, conscious of his own unjustifiable deficiency in that important accomplishment.

"But that you take what to you doth belong
It were a fault to snatch words off my tongue,"

maliciously quoted the lady. "Well, at all events," said Ralegh, looking as angry as a gentleman well could do, "you shall not be troubled with me; I will not dance with you!" "Truly, that will be a loss!" cried Edith; "why I shall never get over the disappointment! Well, well, I must see how charming I can make myself. Perhaps Captain Delaford may ask me a second time." "And there he comes, Madam!" exclaimed Arthur, who saw the very gentleman in question galloping up the avenue. No pleasant sight, for he looked remarkably well on horseback, and the lover saw, or fancied that he saw, Edith watching admiringly. Had he looked a little closer he would have seen that her eyes were filled with tears, and that she had only turned aside to conceal them. But Arthur was too angry to observe. "I will not interrupt your téte à tête, Madam. I now understand why it was too hot to ride with me this morning;" and without waiting for an answer, he sprang from the terrace, and was soon lost to sight among the coppices below. Edith remained to do the honours to her visitor with what grace she might. But anger gave her spirit, and she contented herself with turning in mind the dignified resentment she would display when they met at dinner. Never had Edith looked more beautiful than when she paused on the threshold of the old gothic library, where the guests were assembled for dinner, to still a little fluttering at the heart before she entered the room where she expected to meet Arthur. She entered, a little flush on her cheek, and a little sparkle in her clear blue eyes. Her father came towards her, and drew her arm in his. He was almost as proud as fond of his lovely child. She gave one quick glance round the library. Arthur was not there. Captain Delaford came forward with a smile and a compliment. She scarcely answered him; and it was a positive relief when an old baronet, who had been sent into the world to be a bore, and who from his cradle had fulfilled his destiny, came forward, and handed her to the dinner table. There were one or two late arrivals;—they little knew how quickly the heart of the fair mistress of the house beat at their entrance. The longest dinner that Edith had ever known was at length over;—but a yet longer evening was to come. She went with a large party from their house to the ball, and she danced the first dance with Captain Delaford. Ah, the restraints of society! Her pulses beat feverishly; her eyes were filled with tears; she was anxious—restless; and yet she had to appear gay, polite, and occupied with the scene before her. How often during the course of that evening did she go through a course of manoeuvres to obtain a place near the door, and then, ashamed of her motive, leave it hastily, only to return again! Still Arthur never came.

The party returned to the hall; and it was as much as Edith could do to appear the attentive and well-bred mistress of the house. Generally speaking, the little supper at home, after the dance, had been so gay; to-night it was positively dull—all said they were tired. The visitors took up their candles, and as the door closed upon the last, Edith threw herself into her father's arms and burst into tears. Half in sobs, and half in words, her story was told, and Mr Trevanion was at first very angry with Arthur Ralegh's want of temper. But Edith could not bear to have him blamed, and she now made all sorts of excuses for the jealousy which in the morning seemed to her so unpardonable. It was a lovely night when, feverish and restless, she flung open the windows of her dressing-room. The moon was shining in a cloudless sky, and the sea in the distance was tremulous with light. But there was a weight on Edith's spirits which she could not shake off. The clouds were beginning to redden in the east before she went to bed, and the last words on her lips were, "Where is Arthur?" Where, indeed, was he? When he left Edith he rushed in a paroxysm of rage to the sea-side, and there, bare-headed, he amused himself with walking up and down, cursing woman's fickleness and all good waltzers in his heart. Suddenly a little boat shot round one of the small capes which so gracefully indent the coast, a youth sprang out, and approaching Arthur, unperceived, passed his arm through the wanderer's and addressed him in the well-known

"Why bare-headed are you come,
Or why come you at all!"

It was an old college friend; and Arthur, between anger and confidence, was soon moved to tell his story. "I will tell you what you shall do; come with me into my boat, my yacht waits me in the offing; we will have a pleasant sail, a gay supper, and to-morrow, you, having so shown with what spirit you can act, shall to-morrow go and beg your fair tyrant's pardon—or, what is far better, let her beg your's." Arthur was just in that sort of mood, when we are ready to let anyone decide for us rather than ourselves. He went with his friend, had a gay supper, and did what he could to drown a few of Edith's frowns in Champagne. He woke the next morning with a headache, and the agreeable intelligence that they were driven out to sea. It was a week before they could land; and when they did, of course Arthur's first thought was to hasten to Edith. For this purpose he was put in at the very creek which he had left the day before. "You look so handsome in my foraging cap," said his gay companion, "that you must carry everything before you."

Arthur's step was as heavy as his spirits. He could not disguise from himself that his strange absence must have inflicted a degree of most cruel anxiety, and he dreaded to see Edith again. The sound of the bell tolling for a funeral did not add to his cheerfulness. He had to pass by the little churchyard, and saw a group of people in the one corner. Surely they were gathered round the old vault of the Trevanions. He entered—the rattle of the earth on the coffin struck upon his ear—the vault was open, and the clergyman was reading the last sacred words that part the dead from the living. He asked one question, and the wretched young man heard the name of Edith Trevanion. His sudden disappearance, and his hat having been found on the sea-shore, led to the belief that he had destroyed himself. This report had been hastily communicated to Edith, and she had broken a blood-vessel. Death followed instantly. In the small churchyard, whose old yews are seen at a great distance out at sea, is an old-fashioned monument—it is the vault of the Trevanion family. The last inscription is—

"Edith Trevanion, aged 19."

I never saw a girl for whom the epithet lovely seemed so completely suited as Mildred Pemberton: she was made up of all bright colours. Her lip was of the most vivid scarlet, her cheek of the warmest rose, her eyes of that violet blue so rarely seen except in a child, and her skin of a dazzling white, so transparent, that the azure veins in her temples seemed almost as blue as her eyes. Her hair curled naturally, and no poetical simile ever went beyond the truth of their brightness. Gold, sunshine, &c., were the only comparisons for those glossy ringlets. When she was two-and-twenty she scarcely looked sixteen, and her manners were as childish as her face and figure. She was guileless, enthusiastic, and sensitive; too ignorant in every way both of books and things perhaps to be called clever, but she had in herself all the materials for becoming so: with that quick perception which the imagination always gives, and the energy which is the groundwork of all excellence.

Sir Henry Pemberton, her father, was a severe man, and it was said that a young and beautiful wife had withered in the ungenial atmosphere of his cold stern temper. Only that Englishmen have a travelling mania, and the more comfortable they are at home, the less they can abide to stay there, no one could have accounted for Sir Henry's coming to Rome. He cared nothing for the fine arts. I doubt whether the finest music would have wrung from him more than Dr. Johnson's ejaculation, when the difficulty of some celebrated overture was dwelt upon, "Difficult!—I wish it were impossible." I never heard him make but one remark on painting, namely, "wonder that people should go to so much trouble and expense to have that on canvass, which they see better in the streets any day." For antiquities he had no taste, and society he positively disliked. His daughter, however, had his share of enjoyment and her own too—she was delighted with everything. The poetry of her nature was called forth by the poetical atmosphere of Rome. She had that peculiar organization, on which music has influence like "the enchanter's wand;" while Corinne and Chateaubriand had already excited all her sympathies for "the world of ashes at her feet." But, after seeing her at the Spanish ambassador's ball dancing with the young Count Arrezi, I was persuaded that the fair English girl was investing all things around her with that poetry which the heart flings over the commonplaces of life once "and once only."

A night or two afterwards (for we both lived in the Piazza di Spagna) I heard the chords of a guitar accompanying a song from "Metastasio;" I also heard a window unclose, and then came a few extempore stanzas in honour of a certain wreath of flowers which I took for granted were thrown into the street. Now a guitar, a cloak, moon light, and a handsome cavalier, what nature—at least what feminine nature—could resist them? Accustomed to the seclusion of a country-seat, or the small coterie of a country town, where her taste, feeling, and fancy alike were dormant, the effect of Rome on Mildred Pemberton was like a sudden introduction into fairyland. Her eyes and senses were alike fascinated—she lived in a dream of realized poetry. Love and youth are ever companions, and Mildred was no exception to the general rule. But hers was one of those natures which love affects the most intensely; it was, indeed,

"The worship the heart lifts on high,
And the heavens reject not."

For such love is the emanation of all that is most elevated and most unselfish in our nature. On this subject any general rule is impossible; love, like the chamelion, is coloured by the air in which it lives— and the finer the air the richer the colour. Some young ladies have a happy facility of falling in and out of love; their heart, like a raspberry tart, is covered with crosses. But Mildred was too sensitive and too ideal for these "light summer fancies." Her affection was her destiny, and she loved the young Italian with the devotion and depth of a love that was half poetry. I never saw a handsomer couple—such perfect representatives of the north and south: she, fair as that sweetest of roses, the one called the maiden's blush; and he of that rich dark olive, which suits so well with the high Roman features.

There are always plenty of people to talk of what does not concern them, and a love affair would seem to be everybody's business; precisely because it is one of all others with which they have the least to do. At last the affair reached Sir Henry's ears, and he was as furious as any father in a romance of four volumes; bread and water, and to be locked up for life, were among the least of his menaces. I believe that he thought himself merciful because they were the only ones that he actually inflicted. He was wrong, as all are who rouse the passive resistance of a woman's nature. The indignity and violence with which she was treated only made her turn more fondly to the shelter of the loving heart she believed was so truly her own. Kindness might have brought her to her father's feet, ready to give up her dearest hopes for his sake; but his harsh anger only made her tremble at the hopeless future. There was also another motive which strengthened her resolution, she had become secretly attached to the Catholic faith, and, like all young converts, was enthusiastic in her belief. Love might have something to do with the conversion. Sir Henry said that it had done all the mischief; but Mildred at all events believed, that even had the Count d'Arrezi been out of the question, her vocation would have been the same, still she felt happy in the idea of their mutual conviction.

Well, one moonlight night a closely-shrouded couple were seen gliding across the Piazza di Spagna. The fountain's low and melancholy singing was the only sound, and the moon shone full on the magnificent flight of steps which led to the convent della Trinita de Monti. The stately domes shone like silver in the lovely night, and Mildred ascended the vast steps with the buoyant feet of hope as she gazed upon them. They pointed out her place of refuge, and she was conducted thither by Arrezi. Gradually as she ascended, the singing of the fountain died away in the distance, but a still sweeter song arose on the air. The nuns were at vespers, and the solemn chant pierced even the huge walls by which they were surrounded. Mildred clung to her lover's arm as they paused before the gates; she started at the deep sound of the bell which announced their arrival—it struck like a knell on her heart. Her appearance was expected, and she was at once conducted to the Abbess; a tall, stately woman, but one whose sad brow and cheek worn before its time, told that suffering and sorrow had preceded the quiet of the cloister.

It was with strange feelings that Mildred laid down on the little pallet appointed for her. The room was small and lofty, apparently partitioned off from one of larger size, for the height was quite disproportionate, and the walls were covered with huge frescos, containing passages from the Holy Scriptures; these were abruptly terminated by a dark, carved wainscoting, that stretched on one side. The apartment was singularly gloomy, and the subject of the fresco served anything but to relieve it—it represented the Murder of the Innocents. Not a horror was spared; here a pale, wild-looking woman struggled, but vainly, with the ruffian who could only reach her child through herself; another was flying, but the infant in her arms wore the livid hues of death. To the left a female, whose high and Jewish but handsome features were well suited to the expression of a Judith or a Jared—stood with her arm raised, and her mouth convulsed with the blending of agony and prophecy—apparently in the act of cursing; but the most touching figure of all was a woman kneeling by the bodies of two children, twisted in each other's arms and pierced by the same blow. There was such a fixed look of intense despair in the large tearless eyes, such a stupidity of horror in the set and rigid face—as if every consciousness was gone but that of horror; the eyes of Mildred were riveted upon it. The thought of how strong a parent's affection must be arose in her mind, and at that moment she reproached herself for leaving her father; then the terror of his anger, mingled with tenderness for her lover, combatted her regret. "Oh! that my mother,"—exclaimed she, throwing herself on the rude pallet below, "had lived to counsel and to love me!" And the image of that pale lady seated lonely in her dressing-room, to which she was confined for months before she died, hardened Mildred's heart against her father. She was a little creature of some six years old when Lady Pemberton died; but her wan and lovely countenance, her sweet sad voice, the tears that rose so often unbidden to her faint blue eyes, were to her child as things of yesterday.

At length she slept; but the tears were yet glittering on her long eye lashes when the first rosy gleams of day-break awakened her: she started with that half recollection which attends our first confused arousing—she wondered where she was—the events of the preceding night flashed upon her—she trembled as she thought of the irrevocable step she had taken. The cross was hung at the foot of her pallet, and she flung herself on her knees before it, and a more fervent and unselfish prayer never yet arose to that heaven, where alone is pity and pardon. Her devotions over, she approached the window, and the calm and lovely scene gave its own cheerfulness: the crimson blush of the daybreak was melting around the spires that gleamed on high, and long, soft shadows fell from the ilex and cypress, whose huge size attested the long seclusion of the convent garden. The distant murmur of the little fountain was only broken by the rustle of the birds amid the leaves, and the early chirp of the cicada in the long grass beneath: Mildred felt soothed and cheered, it is so impossible for youth to resist the influence of morning.

Sir Henry was wild with rage when he heard of his daughter's flight. He challenged the Count, who refused to meet the father of his future wife. Next he bent all his efforts towards the recovery of Miss Pemberton; a direct application was made to the Pope, that forcible means might be used for her restoration: this was refused. Miss Pemberton was of age, and the church would not refuse its protection to one about to become a member of its flock.

On receiving this answer, Sir Henry made immediate preparation for leaving Rome; but the morning of his departure he sent for the Count Arrezi. The lover obeyed the summons, supposing that it was some overture to a reconciliation; on his arrival he found Sir Henry pale with suppressed rage, and pacing the hall, at whose entrance the travelling carriage was waiting. Arrezi was somewhat staggered to perceive these signs of actual departure; however, he entered, and was received by his intended father-in-law with a polite bow.

"I have many apologies to make," said the Baronet, with a manner studiously courteous, "for giving you this trouble—but I wished to send by you a message to Miss Pemberton. You understand English, I believe, or my servant can interpret for me?"

"I understand ver vel," said the Count; "shall be too happy to take von message."

"Well then, Sir," continued his companion, "you will inform Miss Pemberton that she is entitled to one hundred a-year left her by her aunt, and that this will be punctually paid in to Torloni's; beyond this she is not to expect a shilling from me. I leave Rome to-day: I will never see her again—never permit her name to be mentioned in my presence. My property will go to my nephew—and all I shall ever leave her will be my curse." So saying, Sir Henry passed the Italian with a low bow, and entered his carriage.

"Holy saints!" exclaimed the Count in Italian, catching hold of the servant's arm, "he cannot mean what he says?"

"If you knew Sir Henry as well as I do," replied the man, "you would not doubt it," and he hurried after his master.

The Count stood as if the carriage had been Medusa's head—"A hundred a-year!" muttered he; "why, my mustachios are well worth that!"

He returned to his house, smoked two cigars, and then repairing to the Convent della Trinita, requested to see the Abbess. "Madam," said he, as soon as the stately superior had taken her seat in the large arm-chair, "there are some unpleasant affairs which are best settled through the intervention of a third person. Will you inform Miss Pemberton that I have seen Sir Henry this morning, who has left Rome, and that he desires me to let her know that the hundred a-year which she inherits will be punctually paid in to Torloni's; but that from himself she never must expect a shilling: he will leave her nothing but his curse. To that," continued the Count, with his most melo-dramatic air, "I will not expose her; I sacrifice myself, and leave Rome to-night. Will you tell her this, and spare both the unutterable agony of farewell?"

"You will excuse my undertaking any such mission," replied the superior, fixing on him her dark and flashing eyes, beneath whose scorn Arrezi felt himself quail for the moment; "you will say what you think proper to the English signora yourself." So saying she rang the silver bell on the table beside, whose summons was instantly obeyed by a novice, and Miss Pemberton's presence was requested in the parlour. The Abbess averted her face and took up her beads, and the Count was left standing by the window to arrange the coming conversation as best he might. A light step was soon heard, and Mildred Pemberton came in, looking lovelier in the simple conventual garb than ever she had done with all the aids of dress; the folds only fastened in at the waist, suited her childish figure. The pure white of the veil was scarcely to be discerned from the pure white of the skin; the single braid of gold on either side her forehead betrayed how rich the hair was that lay concealed—and the small features gave something of the innocence of infancy to her face; a bright blush crimsoned her face as she entered, too shy to extend the little hand to her lover which trembled at her side.

"My angel," said the Count, dropping on one knee, "I have seen your father this morning." Mildred turned deadly pale. "Do not fear—I will give up everything, even yourself, rather than make you wretched. He has threatened our union with his curse. Thus I prevent its falling on you, Mildred—I renounce all claim upon you—I will leave Rome to-night."

Mildred stood white and speechless. A woman whose lover resigns her, and as if for her own sake, though without consulting her, is placed in a most awkward situation. What can she do? Take him at his word? That is easy to say, but hard to do, when all the hopes and affections are garnered in his love. The Superior saw her painful position, and addressed the gentleman.

"You have forgotten to mention, Count Arrezi, that Miss Pemberton will in future receive only the hundred a-year that she inherits from her aunt."

The colour came back to Mildred's cheek and lips; she sought to meet her lover's eye, but it avoided her own. With a woman's quick instinct, where the feelings are concerned, she saw his motives. With a degree of dignity of which her slight form had scarcely seemed capable, she turned calmly to the Abbess, and said,

"Have I your permission that the Count Arrezi will leave us together? It seems to me unnecessary to prolong our last interview."

The Count approached, and began some hurried sentences of good wishes, devotion, sacrifice of his own happiness, &c.; but she interrupted him almost sternly—

"I have but one favour to ask, which is, that you will leave me, and at once."

Glad to have been released on such easy terms, for he had expected prayers, tears, and reproaches, Arrezi instantly obeyed. The door closed after him, and Mildred dropped senseless on the floor. The Abbess called for no assistance, she pitied the agony of the moment too much, to let it be observed. She raised the youthful sufferer in her arms, and bathed her face with essence, and when Mildred recovered, her head rested on the shoulder of the Superior, who was watching her with the tenderness of a mother. "These are the trials, my child, which make us turn to heaven. The holy Madonna keep you!" This was her only remark, and Mildred went to her cell.

It was fortunate for her that her health gave way beneath so much excitement—the body sometimes saves the mind. Next day she was too ill to move, and it was weeks before the fever left her. Of all things time can the least be measured by space. Years, or the effects of years, had passed over the head of Mildred, before she rose from that couch of sickness. She left there the rose of her cheek, the light of her eye—

"Her lip still wore the sweetness of a smile,
But not its gaiety."

The buoyancy of her step, her sweet singing laugh, were gone for ever,—she had lived past youth and hope. Some one has truly said—

"'Tis not the lover which is lost,
    The love for which we grieve,
It is the price that they have cost,
    The memories which they leave."

This was the case with Mildred—she despised Arrezi too thoroughly to regret him—she deeply felt how unworthy he was of her deep-devoted affection. Always accustomed to wealth, she did not understand its value; we must want money to really know its worth, and money seemed to her the vilest consideration that could have influence. She thought with astonishment on the duplicity of the Count. Inconstancy she could have forgiven; that would have come within the limits of her poetical experience. She had been capable of any personal sacrifice to secure his happiness, even with a rival; but to be left so unhesitatingly the moment that she had no longer the prospect of wealth, showed too plainly what his object had been from the first—all his enthusiasm, all his romance, had been mere acting. She shrank away from a world in which there was such deceit. To what could she trust whose confidence had been so betrayed? Mildred Pemberton had laid down on the pallet of her secluded cell a girl full of the confidence, the generous impulses, the warm affections of girlhood; she rose from it a grave and thoughtful woman. She had ceased to look forward, she wished for nothing but quiet, she hoped, but only in heaven. All the poetry of her imaginative temperament flung back violently upon herself, served only to strengthen the influence of her new creed. Beloved by all, the earnestness of her devotion made her thought almost a saint by some; and the sweet, strange accents of the English novice, blending in the hymns of the saintly choir, gave a new fervour to religious exaltation. She entered upon the duties of her new state with zeal, and in their performance, and the thousand chains of daily habit, sought forgetfulness of the past. Still it was hard to forget her native tongue, and her native land. Separated from her father, his harshness was forgotten, and she only remembered the ties that united them.

She had been in the convent nearly a twelvemonth, and the time for the final vows was rapidly approaching, when one day to her astonishment she heard an English voice in the garden, and saw the fair face of one of her own countrywomen. She soon became acquainted with Emily Pemberton, and found that she was her cousin, though from a family disagreement they had never met. Mildred was mistaken in supposing that she was dead to all sense of affection, for her heart warmed at once to her young relative. It was some time before she found courage to speak of the past, and at last she asked about her father.

"He is quite broken by his last illness; pale, emaciated, he is but the shadow of what he was. It is a melancholy thing to see him wander through the dull rooms of the old hall, as if haunted by the memory of those who had once been there." This conversation sunk deep into Mildred's mind, though at the time she could not trust her voice to answer. Again and again it was renewed; at last Mildred hazarded the question—

"Do you think my father would see me?"

"I am sure he would," exclaimed Emily; "it is only pride that prevents him seeking you. But should not that be your part?—you would not have a parent humble himself to his child?"

Before they parted that evening, it was settled that Mildred should accompany her cousin the following week, whither she was returning under the protection of her brother. The fact was, that the moment Sir Henry arrived in England he had sent for his nephew, executed a will in his favour, and was then seized with a violent illness, which truly had left him an altered man. He remembered his harshness to his wife and child now they were both removed from him. He missed Mildred more than he would have owned even to himself. Charles, his nephew, saw all this: from the first announcement of his uncle's intentions he had resolved not to profit by them, and the sight of his drooping spirits confirmed him in a plan he had formed. His sister entered into it with all the romance of youth, and off they set to Rome together, and, as we have narrated, carried their project into effect.

The next morning Mildred requested an audience of the abbess, whose kindness to her from the morning Count Arrezi left the parlour had never known change. She explained to her all her thoughts and feelings; her misery at fancying her father desolate in his old age, and her conviction that she ought to seek his pardon. "If he reject me, I return to your feet, my mother!"

The superior for an instant yielded to the weakness of humanity; tears stood in her eyes, and her stately head rested for a moment on Mildred; but the motion was soon subdued, and the voice was almost as steady as usual, as she said, "Go, my beloved child; your duty to your sick and solitary parent is paramount to every other; in fulfilling that you best fulfil your duty to your God. Go; but if the world again repeat its bitter lessons, and you shrink from a burden too heavy to bear, remember, while I live you have a home in the Convent della Trinita."

Mildred bathed the hand pressed to hers with her tears; they were the truest thanks.

A week more saw the cousins on the road to England, which they traversed with all possible rapidity; and with a throbbing heart Mildred found herself in the Park which she had quitted so many months ago, and yet it seemed like yesterday, for not a sign of change appeared. The sun was sinking over the avenue of old oaks; the lake was reddening with the glow; the long shadows rested on the grass, while in the distance they mingled in undefined obscurity. The deer were gathered together beneath the trees, and a large dog-rose bush was in the full luxuriance of its faint and fragile flower.

Charles Pemberton and his sister went forward to prepare Sir Henry, but after a few moments Mildred's anxiety became uncontrollable. Gradually she approached the house; she ascended the terrace, and, once there, thought that she might safely enter. There was a little room which opened upon it—it had once been her own favourite chamber, for it contained a picture of her mother, with herself, then a little creature of two years old, in her hand. As she approached she heard voices, but the turn in the wall, for it was a corner room, completely concealed her. She stood, not daring to breathe, amid the long tendrils of the honeysuckle. She could not be mistaken—it was her father's voice and she heard him say, "Charles, I own the weakness—I do pine to see my child."

The next moment Mildred was at his feet. She found him much changed; illness had subdued his iron strength. He was lonely and dependent, and he now acknowledged the need of that affection which hitherto he had repelled. He soon could scarcely bear his daughter out of his sight, and she watched his every look. Sir Henry, almost confined to the house, driven about in a pony-chaise, was a happier man than he had ever been. One only subject of anxiety remained—he had openly made his nephew his heir, and he now saw the prior claim of his own child. They were gathered one summer evening in the little parlour, which still continued their favourite room, when Sir Henry introduced the subject. "It does not need," exclaimed the cousins, in a breath.

But Charles had yet more to say; he told Mildred that he loved her, and implored her father to give her hand, as of far more value than all the wealth that he could bequeath. Mildred allowed her hand to rest in his; but even the lover could draw no encouragement from the action. She was calm, but very pale—and her kindness was only kindness. "Charles," said she, looking on with the gentle affection of a sister, "I have loved once—however unworthily, I can never love again. I returned not to the world, but to my home—I am God and my father's!"

Charles gazed earnestly on the sweet eyes that sank not beneath his own. He saw that hope was out of the question, and pressing the hand which he relinquished, would have left the room; but detaining him, she turned to her father, and said, "He is my brother, is he not?"

"It shall be as you wish, Mildred," replied Sir Henry, "though I had hoped otherwise."

Charles soon after left them for a gay season in London, and where he formed an attachment to the beautiful but portionless orphan of an officer who had been killed in the Peninsula; it was Mildred who reconciled Sir Henry to the match. The young couple took up their residence at Pemberton House, and Mildred was to them as a sister.

At Sir Henry's death it was found that he had bequeathed his whole property to his nephew, with only a sufficient annuity to his daughter, and a little cottage which she had had built in the park. This was close to her cousins, without the strict retirement in which she lived being any check upon them. She never married, but passed her life in acts of kindness. Her place was by the sick bed, or with the afflicted,—the soother of every sorrow, the friend in every trouble. The children, who were fast growing up in the old Hall, adored her; and when, in after days, they passed her portrait in the gallery, it was with the same remark—"If ever there was an angel on earth it was my cousin Mildred!"

AN OLD LADY OF THE LAST CENTURY

'Tis an often-quoted adage of the celebrated Jewish "lover, king, and sage," that "there is nothing new under the sun." I think that, in the present day, one might rather say "there is nothing old." We are conjugating the verb change, in all its moods and tenses. Coleridge says—

"For what is grey with age becomes religion."

We are atheists to the past, and act upon Wordsworth's principle, —

"Of old things, all are over-old;
Of good things, none are good enough:
We'll help to show that we can frame
    A world of other stuff."

Trees, streets are passing away as rapidly as their inhabitants, and today has nothing in common with yesterday. Marmontel had "un grand regret pour la fiérie" and I have un grand regret for the old school.

In endeavouring to recall a few memorials of Mrs. Lawrence Burgoyne, I do it on the same principle that scientific men collect the bones of a mammoth—the whole exists no longer; but there are sufficient remains to show that it did exist. The few survivors of the old school, such as are kept alive by having life annuities—a plan which has some secret charm for putting off death—even these few are fast disappearing. Mrs. Burgoyne has been dead these two years; she had borne a great deal. Powder and hoops had been left off, guineas had changed into sovereigns, and, like many other things, lost by the change; but the last shock to her nerves was given by her granddaughter. Miss Ellen, an urchin of some six years old, came to see her grandmother during the Christmas holidays. Mrs. Burgoyne having heard that the child was a quiet one—though she had some misgivings about the matter—prepared a book for her entertainment; it was a volume of Mother Goose's Fairy Tales. Plum cake and sweet wine were duly administered in the first instance, and the cat recommended as a playmate in the second: the cat, however, being declined, the book was produced. The young lady opened the pages—turned them over with a solemn air of contempt—and then, throwing the work aside, begged that "she might have something to read that would improve her mind." Her grandmother never got over the shock—but took to her bed, ejaculating "What will this world come to! Improving her mind at six!—why, at sixteen I did not know whether I had a mind or not!"

Mrs. Burgoyne passed the last twenty years of her life in a large, solemn-looking house at Kensington; it is now a mad-house. How curiously do these changes in dwelling places, once cheerful and familiar, bring the mutability of our existence home! It would be an eventful chronicle, the history of even a few of the old-fashioned houses in the vicinity of London. You ascended a flight of steps, with a balustrade and two indescribable birds on either side, and a large hall, which, strange to say, was more cheerful in winter than in summer. In summer the narrow windows, the black wood with which it was panelled, seemed heavy and dull; but in winter the huge fire gave its own gladness, and had besides the association with old English hospitality which a blazing grate always brings. You passed next through two long drawing-rooms, whose white wainscoting was almost covered with family portraits. There cannot be much said for the taste of Queen Anne's time downwards—bagged, wigged, and hooped; there was not a picture of which the African's question might not have been asked, "Pray tell me, white woman, if this is all you?" The floors were dry-rubbed, and the mahogany tables shone as if in recollection of former festivities, when whole nights floated away like the—

"Hydaspes, dark with billowy wine."

The chairs were high-backed and the seals covered with needle-work: there was also a buffet, through whose glass doors appeared some singularly small tea-cups, and some still more singularly small tea-pots—why, it would take a dozen to fill one of our modern breakfast cups. The third was Mrs. Burgoyne's own room—and here comfort had made some encroachment on precedent; indeed it was needed by her bodily weakness. The room was carpeted—books and various trifles were on the table, and in an arm-chair was seated the old lady herself: her tall figure was still unbent, and the aristocratic hand was still white: she had no peculiarity of costume, unless it was its extreme propriety—she was, indeed, the very beau-ideal of black satin and blonde. I think it cost her the bitterest pang of all to part with her train, it was like going a grade lower in society. Still, to use her own remark, "It is better to be anything rather than conspicuous: never meet the fashion, but always follow it." She had been a beauty and an heiress, and had gone through life on the sunny side. Tombstones had been her only monitors; but the deep sorrow of death brings with it deep sympathy. Opposite to her were hung the portraits of her husband and her only daughter, whom she had lost very young; but for such humanizing distress, her nature might have been hardened in its glittering course of worldly prosperity—but with her, the well of tears had opened too deeply ever to dry again. On a little ebony table at her elbow were placed her bible and prayer-book, in which she read the psalms and lessons every morning; a friend fancying it was bad for her eyes, somewhat foolishly remonstrated, and asked if she had always done so? "My dear," said the old lady, "youth forgets what age never does—its Maker."

Mrs. Burgoyne was cheerful, and fond of society; in the morning she had a levée of visiters, and twice a week at least, a little circle gathered round her of an evening. Then she was seen to advantage. Someone says of cleanliness, that it is next to godliness—the same might be said of politeness. Mrs. Burgoyne's good-breeding was the most perfect thing in the world—I cannot even imagine her saying or doing a rude thing; I do not believe that she ever even thought one. Her manner was as polished and as minutely finished as the carving on an ivory card case: a little stately it might be, and her curtsey belonged to the days of hoops and brocades—her curtsey was the only old fashion she could not give up—still it put you at your ease; she knew well how to encourage, and she had too much good taste, I might add good feeling, ever to patronize. There never was a more exquisite listener; with what graceful patience would she endure the most wearisome stories—with what quickness catch the least attempt at wit, often giving the said attempt some nice turn, of which the originator was quite guiltless—not that she was the least of a bel esprit. She spoke with admiring deference of Mrs. Montagu and Mrs. Carter's coteries, but she had never belonged to them; she had just the most delicate dread in the world of being called clever. Indeed it is a doubtful fact whether clever people are ever very agreeable; they are too much absorbed by one particular pursuit, too bound lightly enough over those generalities which are the stepping-stones of conversation; they feel as if they ought to say something worth remembering. Now carelessness in the talker is what most puts the listener at ease with himself. In some cases it seems a duty to recollect, and we all know what disagreeable things duties are.

Mrs. Burgoyne, on the contrary, was simple and naïve to the age of eighty. Her talents had never been overlaid; indeed she used to enjoy quoting a speech which the Duchess d'Abrantes puts into the mouth of her mother, the prettiest and most fascinating femme à la mode that ever took her degrees la haute science of French coquetterie. Mde. de Permon says, "Je n'ai jamais lue d'ouvrage plus grave que

Télémaque, et je ne suis pas trop ennuyeuse moi!" Our kind hostess rarely stirred from her arm-chair; but that served as an excuse to draw near to herself any one who needed encouragement: none but those who have keen feelings of their own can enter into those of others, and this susceptibility in her was cultivated by that constant attention which is the most difficult lesson of good breeding. Mrs. Burgoyne was proud—but her very pride showed itself in respect—she only claimed what she herself was ready to yield: her theory was comprised in her favourite anecdote of the late Lord Besborough. While getting into his carriage one day, a poor woman asked charity; he gave her a shilling, but it dropped into the mud: he instantly stooped down, picked it up, and wiped it with his handkerchief before he put it into her hand.

The little circle that used to gather round her is now dispersed—the loss of Mrs. Lawrence Burgoyne has been felt by many; sympathies and affections lingered with her to the last. I know no one remaining the least like her. The vault of her Norman ancestors has closed over the kindest friend and the most thorough-bred gentlewoman.

A FRIEND IN NEED IS A FRIEND INDEED

"There is nothing in the papers, and nobody in the streets," said Charles Bouverie, as with a disconsolate air he flung down the 'Times,' and turned away from the window. "I may as well write to Audley-place, and say that they must kill their own partridges this year; I can't leave town." Charles went towards the table, but he had no lady-like powers of filling four sheets with nothing, and the letter was soon sealed. Again he was thrown upon his resources; which have always appeared to me the very worst things on which an unfortunate individual can be thrown in the way of amusement. He looked round the room: there was one gentleman asleep—Charles envied him; and another reading the third side of a newspaper,—he was one of those who never omit even an advertisement—the fourth side yet remained, and Charles envied him too. The fact was, that though, of course, it is the most enviable position in the world, that of having nothing to do, yet one requires to be used to it. Now our hero had been accustomed to the very reverse. Left an orphan to the care of three uncles,—the first intended him for a clergyman; saw to his Latin, Greek, and Hebrew; and fully impressed upon his nephew's mind the paramount importance of University honours. However, he died; and the second uncle insisted on the senior wrangler taking a place in his counting-house. A will of his own in a young man without a shilling is a superfluity, and Charles took his place on a high stool at a high desk. Just then the third uncle died. He had troubled his head very little about "the only hope of the family" during his life; but after all, the last recollections are often the best, and he recollected his nephew to some purpose. Charles Bouverie was left sole heir to a fine fortune; for the elder Mr. Bouverie died just as he had realized the sum on which he meant to enjoy himself. To the best of our belief, he had seen the pleasure; for the enjoyment of spending money is nothing to that of making it. Charles gave up the ledger as he had given up Euclid; removed to an hotel in the gayer part of town; devoted his mornings to the club instead of the counting-house; and intended to be the happiest men, in the full indulgence of the dolce far niente. Unfortunately, the art of doing nothing requires some learning; and Charles, though he would not have owned the truth on any account, was the least in the world puzzled what to do with himself. London was very empty, and he had as yet but few acquaintance; while he could not help regretting his annual visit at Audley-place. A month of partridges and pheasants is a very real pleasure to a young man country-bred—and forced to spend the other eleven in town.

Our hero approached the window,—that resource of the destitute. There was nothing to be seen, even in St. James's-street! Three hackney-coaches, and two women in pattens passed by; also a man with an umbrella dripping, which he held rather over a brown paper parcel than himself: at last, a bright spot appeared just above the palace, the rain seemed to melt into luminous streaks on the sky, and the rain-drops that had sprinkled all over the panes of glass began to gather into two or three large drops, and to descend slowly along the surface. They would have done to bet upon, but there was no one to bet with. The pavement began to dry, and Charles decided on a walk. He reached the clubs, and stood there for five minutes deliberating whether he should turn to the right hand or to the left, having no necessity for turning to either; and here we cannot but say that necessity is "an injured angel." He, she, or it—is never but harsh, stern, and unpitying; and "cruel necessity" is the phrase par distinction of all parted lovers. Now I hold that necessity merits more amiable adjectives;—what a great deal of trouble is saved thereby. To an undecided person like myself, the inevitable is invaluable. Before Charles had done standing like Hercules in the allegory between Pleasure and Virtue, alias the right and left of St. James's-street—a cabriolet drove rapidly up to the door.

"My dear fellow!" said its occupier, "I am in search of you. I want you to go down with me to my aunt's, and stay there till Wednesday. Her house is within three miles of Croydon, so you could be back in town at an hour's notice. Let me take you to your hotel, and thence I shall get you to drive me down."

Charles accepted the offer with the gratitude of a desperate man; it was just what suited him, and he sprung into the cabriolet in the gayest spirits. Horace Langham, the knight who thus had delivered him for the dragon ennui, had long been the object of his especial envy. He was a young man about town, good-looking, well dressed, with all the externals of a gentleman, quite unquestionable. The few needful preparations were soon made, and as they settled themselves in the stanhope, Langham said, "I have made you drive us down, for my horse has been overworked lately. My aunt unluckily has a great prejudice against strange servants; but there is a nice little country-inn close by, so yours will do very well."

The conversation was for a time very animated, for Horace knew something about every one who was anybody; and was very well inclined to tell all he knew. Anecdotes though, like other treasures, must come to an end; and Charles took advantage of a pause to ask if Mrs. Langham had any family.

"Only a niece," was the reply.

"Is she pretty?" asked his companion.

"Not if you put it to my conscience," said the other; "but she is likely to be rich: will that do as well?"

Charles coloured, from "a complication of disorders." First he was quite shy enough to be annoyed at its being supposed that he cared whether there were any young ladies in the world or not; and, secondly, he was quite romantic enough to be shocked at the idea of money supplying the want of a pretty face. He was relieved from his embarrassment by Mr. Langham's snatching the reins from his hand, and exclaiming, "Bouverie, we must drive back to town immediately! I have forgotten my aunt's netting silk—she will never forgive me!—old ladies are so cursedly unreasonable. Why did she plague me about her horrid silks? However, if we make haste, we shall yet be in time for dinner.—I wonder why old women are left in the world!"

Without waiting for Charles's reply, he put the horse to its utmost speed, and drove furiously back to town. The drive was now any thing but agreeable: a heavy shower of rain beat directly in their faces, and Horace's conversation was confined to maledictions on all elderly gentlewomen, and lamentations on his own ill-luck, in having any thing to do with them. The particular shop was reached; the silk was procured, and again they took the road to Croydon.

The rain continued to fall in torrents, and Langham's spirits seemed to have fallen with the barometer. In sullen silence he continued to drive at a furious rate, till Bouverie's sympathies were awakened on behalf of his horse: he was just about "to hint a fault and hesitate dislike," when the clock of a church in the distance struck six.

"It is of no use now," exclaimed the impatient driver, slackening his speed. "We are too late for dinner,—the thing of all others that puts my aunt out; I must lay the blame upon you, she can't say anything to you as a stranger. We must go and dine at that confounded inn."

Wringing wet, they arrived at a disconsolate-looking inn, 'The Swan.' Truly such a sign only could have swung in such weather. A fire was hastily lighted in the best parlour, from whence the smoke drove them; and they took refuge in the kitchen redolent with the smell of recently fried onions, varied with tobacco; for two men sat on one side the fire employed with two pipes. A very tough beefsteak was produced after some delay, badly dressed, for the chimney smoked; this was washed down with some execrable wine,—half cape, half brandy, but called 'sherry.' Charles could far better have endured these minor discomforts than his companion's ill-humour. Controlled towards himself, it broke with double fury on the heads of the landlady and the kitchen-maid. Charles wondered at this in a man whom he had always seen so full of gaiety and good-humour; but Charles had still many things to learn.

Dinner over, time given for "my aunt's afternoon nap not to be disturbed," they set off for the 'Manor-House,' as it was called. The rain was quite over, but the glistening drops on the green sprays of the hawthorn and ash reflected the moonlight, which was now breaking through the masses of dark cloud. A sweet breath came from the late primroses and the early violets in the hedges of the lane through which they had to pass. Had Bouverie been alone he could have loitered on his way; but his companion had long since merged the poetical in the sarcastic,—if the former quality had ever entered into his composition. They soon arrived at the place of their destination, and entered by a picturesque old gate overhung with ivy; a gravel-walk, and a few stone steps, led into the hall. A sedate-looking butler met them there, and said, with a tone and air equally solemn, "Mrs. Langham, my mistress, waited dinner for you one quarter of an hour; the Major's rice was sadly overdone."

"No fault of mine, my good Williams, I assure you," exclaimed Langham, hurrying on to the sitting-room.

It was large, square, and dark; and a voice, that seemed to Charles singularly shrill, came from the upper end,—"Caroline, my dear, you have spilt the water."

He had no time for further observation, when he was led up to a very tall, upright-looking old lady, in a very tall, upright arm-chair, and was presented in turn to Mrs. Langham, her brother, Major Fanshawe, and to Miss Langham. "Horace," said the old lady, "you kept us waiting dinner a whole quarter of an hour."

"Yes," continued the Major, "and my rice was done to a jelly."

"It was no fault of mine," cried the nephew; "there stands the real culprit. Mr. Bouverie forgot his dressing-case, and we had to drive back for it."

Mrs. Langham's face lost the courteous smile it had summoned up to receive the stranger, and the Major turned aside with a look which said, as plainly as a look could say—and looks speak very plainly sometimes—"What effeminate puppies young men of the present day are!"

Between rage and confusion, Charles could hardly find his way to a seat, where he sat—

"In angry wonder, and in silent shame"

There was, however, no occasion for him to talk. Horace led the conversation, and was very amusing; though, unfortunately for Charles, he had already heard both the scandal and the stories during their drive down. He employed his time in taking a survey of the party. Major Fanshawe was a well-preserved, military-looking man; and it gave him at least ten minutes' consideration to decide whether he wore a wig or not. At last he came to the conclusion that it was the most natural-looking wig that he had ever seen. The old lady took up less time: she seemed staid and severe; and he turned to the younger one. She took up even less time; for the urn almost hid her face, and all he could distinguish was a huge quantity of curls. Now, if there was one thing he hated more than another it was a crop. Like most young men who have always some divinity for the time being whereby to judge of "common mortals," he had his standard of perfection, and Giulietta Grisi reigned at this moment his "fancy's queen." Her small classic head put to shame what he somewhat irreverently called, in his own mind, "a mop of hair." Any little interest that might yet have remained was put to flight; when, at length, after many efforts, he hazarded a question—"Do you play?" and the reply was a single, stiff, hard-hearted "No." Now, a young lady without music was, in his eyes, like a flower without perfume. Matters were made still worse when the tea-things were removed, and she drew towards her a large wicker-basket, from whence peeped out flannel, calico, tape, &c. Charles turned away his head, and encountered an encouraging look from the Major who had drawn nearer towards him. Fanshawe began to talk of the weather; and his auditor was fairly astonished to find how much he had to say about it. He had all but counted the rain-drops; and he was quite aware of every gleam of sunshine that they had had since the morning. He then communicated the important fact that the Manor House fronted due south, and that it was situated on an eminence, which rendered it perfectly dry. "Very necessary for an old house like this. Our house, Sir, is a very old one;—it has the reputation of a ghost. By the bye, that puts me in mind of a very curious— indeed, I may say uncommon—circumstance which happened to me when I was a boy. I was about eight—no, let me see, I was nearly nine. Yes, it was nine; for my birth-day is in February, and the event to which I allude happened in November. Well,—for I am sure you must be impatient for the story young people always like ghost stories,—I had been in bed some time. My father always insisted on our going soon to rest. You know the old proverb,

'Early to bed, early to rise,
Makes a man healthy, and wealthy, and wise.'—

I had been in bed some time. Perhaps I had gone to sleep a little later than usual; for it was a stormy night, and I never was a sound sleeper. My digestion is not good: I am therefore obliged to be very regular in my hours. Your dressing-case, Sir, did me a great deal of harm to-day;—we waited dinner half an hour, and the rice was overdone. However, I always make great excuses for young people. When I was a youth, I was somewhat of a coxcomb myself; indeed, I think, at any time of life, people should never be indifferent to their appearance. I often tell my sister and niece they are too careless.—But I am keeping your curiosity on the rack all this time. So, to return to my story. I had been asleep some time, when I was suddenly awakened by what appeared to me a violent blow on the chest. I started up in my bed; I could perceive no one, though the rushlight was still burning.—We were always allowed a rushlight.—I jumped up, and ran to my mother's dressing-room; I heard the clock strike twelve, as I thought, though afterwards it turned out to be only eleven. Still, as you may easily suppose, it added to my alarm; for twelve o'clock is, as you know, a disagreeable time to be thinking of ghosts—it being the hour peculiarly appropriated to their appearance. However, I communicated my alarm in perfect safety, and my bedchamber was carefully searched, without discovering the slightest cause for fear. My father was a little inclined to be angry; but, as my mother justly observed, there were many things for which there was no accounting. You see, my dear young friend,"—the Major's heart had quite warmed to his patient listener,—"I may well quote Shakspeare's profound remark, which may have escaped your notice hitherto,—

'There are more things in heaven and earth, Horatio,
Than are dreamed of in your philosophy.'

Charles was saved the painful necessity of a reply, by a call on his attention from the other part of the room, and hearing his friend saying, "Oh, Bouverie is a capital tredille player; he used to play it with his uncle. It is the very game for a small circle in the country."

Our hero could not deny the fact—for a fact it actually was;—but how it had reached Langham was to him matter of great surprise. Down he sat to the table with Mrs. Langham and the Major, to devote the rest of the evening to spadille, manille, and basto. At ten, the tray came in, with refreshments much lighter than were ever meant to follow a dinner bad as his own had been; but, as the Major observed, "suppers were so bad for the digestion." At half-past ten, bed-candles were brought in, and "we breakfast punctually at eight" was formally announced by Mrs. Langham.

To bed he went—hungry, weary, but not the least sleepy; and he lay awake, thinking whether it would be possible to return to London the next morning. He was the last to make his appearance; for he had divers misgivings respecting a tête-à-tête with Fanshawe, who he saw at once had that worst bump developed that can adorn the head of a bore—viz., long-story-tellativeness. He entered: Miss Langham's face was again hidden by the urn; but he had a side view of "that odious crop." Mrs. Langham inquired, with old-fashioned politeness, how he had passed the night; so did the Major. "Saw no ghosts?" and forthwith recommenced of "a most curious, I may say unaccountable, thing which happened to me when I was a little boy." It was long enough the previous evening; but at breakfast it was interminable, being ever and anon interrupted by spoonsful of egg;—"An egg is very light; I always eat one at breakfast;"—and by slices of toast, accompanied with "Never touch new bread; but toast is easily digested." A light, however, was thrown on the motive of their visit; for Horace was evidently aux petites soins with Caroline Langham.

After breakfast, all looked towards the windows; but the rain was pitiless, and the sky was of that sombre and unbroken dulness which bespeaks a whole day's rain, at least. The Major challenged Charles to a game at chess, of which nothing worse need be said, than that it began before ten, and lasted till half-past four; when, saying that it could be finished the next day, his opponent hurried Charles off with an injunction to try and dress in time for dinner.

He was dressed in ample time, for he had no motive to linger on the pleasant duties of the toilette—the only duties that I know of to which the term pleasant can be applied. The dinner was certainly the very perfection of a plain dinner, and to that Charles chiefly devoted his attention, taking especial care not to divert Miss Langham's attention from Horace's whispers by any indiscreet questions. The evening was again ruled by those three Fates, Spadille, Manille, and, Basto—but as they were separating for the night, Charles said to his friend, "Of course the least you can do for me will be to ask me to the wedding?"

Horace laughed, and said, "Well, poor little thing—I suppose I must take pity upon her some day or other. One comfort is, that when she is my wife, she cannot be so very fond of me."

No man likes to hear of the conquest of another, and Charles made no effort to prolong the conversation. The next morning was bright, as if the day were as glad as himself of their coming departure. He also most ingeniously out-manoeuvered the Major, by first approaching the window to admire the garden; next stepping out upon the turf, and then walking off as fast as he could, resolved that he would not be found till two-o'clock, when the stanhope was ordered to the door. The day was delightful—the sunshine entered into the spirits, and the soft warm air was freighted with odours from a garden prodigal in sweets.

From the flower-garden he wandered into a little wilderness which communicated with an orchard. Charles paused for a moment to admire the cherry-trees, covered with fruit, whose yellowish green was just beginning to wear a tinge of red on the side next the sun; when suddenly he espied the Major—gun in hand. He then remembered that he had been vowing vengeance against the sparrows at breakfast. The morning was too lovely to waste on stories of—"When I was a little boy;" so he darted behind a tree, and prepared to make his escape unseen. Now, whether his stir among the branches disturbed the birds, or whether the Major thought that he had carried his gun quite long enough without discharging it, we know not; but at that moment he fired. Charles received the shot in his leg, and, stumbling against a tree, struck his head with such violence, that he fell stunned on the ground. When he recovered his senses he found himself in bed, with a gentleman at his elbow, who allowed no one but himself to speak.

On this part of our narrative we need not dwell—but the unfortunate visitor was confined for a week to his bed. The fever under which he suffered rendered even an attempt to amuse him dangerous; but before the week was over he had learned to think Mrs. Langham the kindest old lady in the world; and that the Major was to be endured, now that he was not allowed to say above five words at a time. He had also discovered that Miss Langham had a low sweet voice, and the light step of a sylph. He was pronounced equal to sitting up for a few hours; it is almost worth while to be an invalid for the sake of that permission.

"We placed you in this room at Caroline's suggestion," said Mrs. Langham; "it is the one which she occupies, and opens into her own little morning room. As she very justly observed, you could then have change, the moment it was needed, without any fatigue."

Accordingly he was wheeled on the sofa into the adjoining apartment, and left for a little while to recover from the exertion, with an assurance that she and her niece would soon be with him. Charles took the opportunity of looking about him; and the survey very much raised Miss Langham in his estimation.—there was so much feminine taste in the arrangement of the various trifles scattered round. There was a pretty and well-furnished bookcase: he read the titles on the backs of several, and perceived both French and Italian authors mingled with the English. A number of engravings hung on the walls, all chosen with reference to their subjects, all of which had a little touch of sentiment. Some fresh flowers, grouped as only those who have an eye for colours can group them, were upon the table, and a basket of choice plants was in the window; a guitar rested on a stand of music; in short, nothing was wanting that Charles deemed essential in a lady's room. He was not left long to his meditations—his hostess and her niece re-appeared, and he was soon engaged in a very pleasant conversation.

Mrs. Langham was called suddenly away; and for a few minutes there was a pause—broken by Charles asking the young lady—"If she had any friends that were musical?"

"No," replied Caroline. "Indeed we have very few neighbours; my aunt has outlived most of her own friends, and is reluctant to make new ones. We see few strangers, excepting an acquaintance whom Horace now and then brings down—or some old companions of my uncle's."

There was something in the familiar appellation "Horace" that jarred on Charles's ear—and there was another pause: after which he could think of nothing better to say, than—

"Mr. Langham is a very gentlemanlike young man!"

"Do you think so," replied his companion coldly.

Charles tried to get a glance at her face, but it was hidden by the curls which fell forward as she bent over her knitting.

"And very witty," continued Bouverie.

"Nay," said Caroline, "there I cannot agree with you. Ridicule is not wit. He is amusing, for he goes a great deal into society, and retails all he there collects—but I never heard him make an original remark in my life."

"He seems, however, a great favourite of yours!" exclaimed the invalid, hastily. "Ah, well!" returned the young lady; "I do not wish to under-value your friend—I see you are half affronted—but a favourite of mine my cousin never was, nor never can be. He is far too selfish."

Charles felt a most ungenerous sensation of pleasure, which however he checked, and magnanimously resolved to change the subject.

"I wonder at seeing a guitar," said he, "as you say you have no musical friends?"

"I do not keep my guitar," replied Caroline, laughing, "for my friends—but for myself!"

"But of what use is it to you?" asked the invalid.

"Not of much use, certainly; but a great deal of pleasure!"

"Pleasure!—what pleasure?"

"Oh, you may not be fond of music—but I am."

"Still, as you do not play it—I do not comprehend the good of the instrument."

"But I do play it!" interrupted Caroline.

"Why!" exclaimed Charles, "you told me, the first evening, that you did not play!"

"Ah, I thought that you meant tredille!"

Bouverie almost sprang from the sofa.

"My dear Miss Langham, I am so passionately fond of music; do lay by your knitting and take your guitar!"

"With pleasure, if it will keep you quiet!" So saying, with equal grace and simplicity, she began to sing an Italian barcarolle.

The light fell on her face, which was turned towards her listener, who perceived for the first time how very pretty it was. The fact was, that he had never looked at her before. We need pursue the subject no farther:—a lady—a guitar—and a wounded cavalier—can have but one denouement—a declaration— and it came in due time; that is, before the week was out.

"You must let me speak to your aunt," said Charles Bouverie, the morning after.

"My dear aunt!" said Caroline, blushing one of those sweet bright blushes which so soon forsake the cheek; "you must not mind a little opposition at first."

"She favours Mr. Langham then?"

"Certainly not;" but colouring still more deeply, "your want of fortune—!"

"My want of fortune!" cried Charles; "why I am all but a millionaire!"

The matter was soon explained. Horace had brought his friend down half as a convenience—half as a foil—and to prevent any possible danger, had represented him as poor: all mistakes were soon cleared up. Settlements and diamonds—blond and britska were arranged with all possible despatch; and Mr. and Mrs. Bouverie were soon announced as "the happy pair, gone during the honey-moon to Paris." The only regret heard on the subject was one expressed by Horace Langham—"Very provoking a man must not marry his aunt! Now that Caroline is so well provided for, my aunt is a speculation well worth consideration."

THE BRIDE OF LINDORF

Midnight is a wonderful thing in a vast city—and midnight was upon Vienna. The shops were closed, the windows darkened, and the streets deserted—strange that where so much of life was gathered together there could be such deep repose; yet nothing equals the stillness of a great town at night. Perhaps it is the contrast afforded by memory that makes this appear yet more profound. In the lone valley, and in the green forest, there is quiet even at noon—quiet, at least, broken by sounds belonging alike to day and night. The singing of the bee and the bird, or the voice of the herdsman carolling some old song of the hills—these may be hushed; but there is still the rustle of the leaves, the wind murmuring in the long grass, and the low perpetual whisper of the pine. But in the town—the brick and mortar have no voices of their own. Nature is silent—her soft, sweet harmonies are hushed in the great human tumult—man, and man only, is heard. Through many hours of the twenty-four, the ocean of existence rolls on with a sound like thunder—a thousand voices speak at once. The wheels pass and re-pass over the stones—music, laughter, anger, the words of courtesy and of business, mingle together—the history of a day is the history of all time. The annals of life but repeat themselves. Vain hopes, vainer fears, feverish pleasure, passionate sorrow, crime, despair, and death—these make up the eternal records of Time's dark chronicle. But this hurried life has its pauses—once in the twenty-four come a few hours of rest and silence.

Vienna was now still as the grave, whose darkness hung over a few lamps swung dimly to and fro, and a few dark shadows—which the crimes of men make needful. The weary watchers of the night paced with slow and noiseless steps the gloomy streets. God knows that many of those hushed and darkened houses might have many a scene of waking care within—many a pillow might be but a place of unrest for the aching head—still the outward seeming of all was repose.

One house, and one only, obeyed not the general law. It was a magnificent hotel in the largest square, and was obviously the scene of a splendid fête. Light and music streamed from the windows, the courtyard was filled with equipages, and a noisy crowd—part servants, part spectators—thronged the gates. Within, all was pomp and gaiety. The Countess von Hermanstadt was unrivalled in her fêtes. She knew how to give them—a knowledge very few possess. The generality labour under the delusion, that when they have lighted and filled their rooms, they have done their all. They never were more in error. Lighting is much—crowding is much also—but there lacks "something more exquisite still." This something the countess possessed in its perfection. Any can assemble a crowd, but few can make it mingle. But Madame von Hermanstadt had a skill which a diplomatist might have studied. She saw—she heard everything; she knew who would and who would not understand each other; she caught at a glance the best position for one lady's velvets, and for the diamonds of another; she never interrupted those who were engaged—she never neglected those who were not; she took care that great people should be amused, and little people astonished. Moreover, she had an object in whatever she did—hence the incentive of interest was added to the pride of art.

The ball of to-night was given in honour of Pauline von Lindorf, her niece, who had just left the convent of St. Therese;—her education, as it is called, completed—that education which is but begun. How many cares—how much sorrow will it take to give the stern and bitter education of actual life! Pauline had just finished a waltz, having pleaded fatigue sooner than might have been expected from a foot so light—a form so fairy-like. She wore a robe of white satin, trimmed with swansdown; large pearls looped back the folds, and a band of diamonds scarcely restrained the bright hair that fell over her neck and shoulders in a thousand natural ringlets. It was of that rare rich golden so seldom seen—almost transparent, like rain with the sunbeams shining through it. At the first glance, that slight and graceful girl—with the rose on her cheek a little flushed by exercise, her glittering curls falling round her, golden as those of Hope—might have seemed the very ideal of youth and pleasure;—so much for the first glance, and how few go beyond! But whoso had looked closer would have seen that the soft red on the cheek was feverish; and there was that tremulous motion of the lip which bespeaks a heart ill at ease. At first she was looking down, and the long shadow of the curled eyelash rested on the rounded cheek; but there was something in the expression of the eyes, when raised, that caught even the most careless passer-by. They were large—unusually large—and of that violet blue which so rarely outlast the age of childhood, while they wore that wild and melancholy look whose shadows have a character of fate;—they are omens of the heart.

It was growing late, and a furtive gaze of the young baroness wandered more and more frequent round the rooms, and each time sought the ground with a deeper shade of disappointment. The Countess von Hermanstadt observed the look, and her own haughty brow curved with a scarcely perceptible frown. It was smoothed away instantly; and passing with a bland smile through the assembled groups, she left the ball-room.

The upper part of the magnificent house was in darkness, but in one window burned a still and lonely lamp. It lighted a small chamber sufficiently removed from the scene of the festival to be quite undisturbed by its tumult, though a distant sound of music floated in, ever and anon, at the open window. The chamber was panelled with old carved oak, and the arches thus formed were filled with books. Books, too, of all sizes, were piled on the ground, and papers and writing materials covered a table in the middle. There were also some pictures: a sombre landscape of Salvator Rosa—just a desolate rock, grey and barren, standing out amid old dark trees, where many a branch was bare with the lightning's fiery visitings. Beneath them stood a single figure—pale, bareheaded, with long black hair that had not yet lost the motion of the wind. He looked what he was—an outlaw; the blood which he had shed, yet warm upon his hand, and his foot yet quivering with its flight for life or death. Near this was a dark, grave portrait by Velasquez: one of those faces whereon time has written the lesson of the prophet king—"All is vanity and vexation of spirit." Others were scattered round, but all more or less of a sombre character, and marking the taste of their possessor. He was a young man of some twenty-two years of age. The richness of part of his costume ill suited the apparently studious recluse; but the task of dressing had been hastily suspended. He had flung a loose robe of sables around him, and leaned back in a large arm-chair, thinking of anything but the festival for which he had begun to prepare. His eye sometimes dwelt on an old history of chivalry, whose silver clasps lay open before him—sometimes on the last sparks of the fire that was dying away on the hearth, but oftener on a copy of a well known Italian picture, the portrait of Beatrice Cenci.

"Yes," said he, half aloud, "a few links bring all life before us: here is adventure—excitement—the toil and the triumph of the body. I wish I had been born in those stirring times—life spent half on horseback, half at the banquet board—when you had but to look round the tournament, fix on the brightest smile, and then win your lady with your sword. Action—action in the sunshine—passion—but little feeling, and less thought: such was meant to be our existence. But we refine—we sadden and we subdue—we call up the hidden and evil spirits of the inner world—we wake from their dark repose those who will madden us. The heart is like the wood on yonder flickering hearth: green and fresh, haunted by a thousand sweet odours, bathed in the warm air, and gladdened by the summer sunshine—so grew it at first upon its native soil. But nature submitteth to art, and man has appointed for it another destiny: it is gathered, and cast into the fire. It seems, then, as if its life had but just begun. A new spirit has crept into the kindled veins—a brilliant light dances around it—it is bright—it is beautiful—and it is consumed! What remains?—A warmth on the atmosphere soon passing away, and a heap of blackened ashes! What more will remain of the heart?"

At this moment a burst of sudden flame sprung up from the mouldering embers, and fell with singular effect on the wan and lovely likeness of Beatrice Cenci. "Why does that face haunt me?" exclaimed the youth. "Why, when others younger and brighter are near, does it glide between them and me like a shadow? I remember finding it as a child in the old deserted gallery. I loved it then, I know not why—save that it brought to my memory a face I fancy watched my sleep when I was a little child. I recollect a large, dark room—a bed whose gloomy curtains were drawn aside—and some one bent over me and kissed me. I put my arms around her neck, and went to sleep, for I had been afraid. She came every night then; but my memory is faint and confused—I can recall nothing more. How beautiful is that picture, with its clear, colourless cheek—with the imperial brow, and the large black eyes filled with melancholy tenderness! Holy Madonna, what a destiny was hers!—A childhood whose sweetest affections were crushed! I can fancy the little pale trembler crouching beneath her angry father's fierce eyes; and at last, as if those soft eyes grew desperate gazing on their slain, who shall say what madness of despair led to the fearful crime—avenging one yet more fearful? Why do I keep it here? It makes me sad—too sad!" And he turned aside, and leant his head upon his hand.

Ernest, for such was the young student's name, was singularly handsome; but it was the heart and the mind that gave their own nameless charm. The heart sent the flushed crimson to the cheek—the mind lighted up the clear white forehead, around which darkened the blackest hair: that deep black hair whose comparisons are all so gloomy, the poet likens it to midnight—to the shadow of the grave—to the tempest—to the raven's wing. Brought from the south, our cold climes just serve to dash the passionate temperament which it indicates with the despondency and the reverie of our sad and misty skies. All women would have called him interesting—the woman who loved him would have called him beautiful. Had the word fascinating never been used before, it would have been invented for him. Like all of his susceptible organization, Ernest was very variable: sometimes the life of society, with every second word an epigram; at others, grave and absorbed—no stimulus, no flattery, could rouse him to animation. His intimate, his very few intimate friends, said that nothing could exceed his eloquence in graver converse: carried away by his feelings, how could he help being eloquent? He was made of all nature's most dangerous ingredients: he thought deeply—he felt acutely; and for such this world has neither resting-place nor contentment.

The door of Ernest's chamber suddenly opened, and its threshold was crossed by a step that certainly had never crossed it before. Stately and slow, as usual, the Countess von Hermanstadt just raised her robe with an air of utter disdain, as she swept by the heavy folios that lay scattered on the ground.

"What! not dressed yet, Ernest?—Certainly the Count von Hermanstadt is well employed, sitting there like a moonstruck dreamer. Pray, am I to have the distinguished honour of a poet or a painter, or,"—added she, pointing sneeringly to a volume of planetary signs that lay open at her feet—"or even an astrologer, as my son?"

Ernest coloured, and rose hastily from his seat. "I do so hate," said he, "those crowds where no one cares for the other; where—"

"No one," interrupted the Countess, "can be so great a simpleton as yourself. Who, in a crowd or elsewhere, will care about one whom they never see? What friends will you ever make in this little, miserable room? The Archduke Charles has twice inquired after you. I managed as well as I could; but I really have something else to do to-night than just to make excuses for you."

"Ah! my mother, you cannot think how unfitted I am for the mock gaiety to-night. Let me stay where I am."

"Nonsense!—Why, there has been your pretty cousin waiting, till I forbade it, to dance with you. I left her waltzing with Prince Louis."

"The less need of me."

"Nay, my dear child!" said his mother, in those caressing tones she well knew how to assume, "think what a slight it will be to our guests if you do not appear; and so many old friends of our house among them. I want assistance. Come, Ernest, would you be the only son in Vienna who would refuse his mother the slight favour of appearing at a ball which is given to introduce him to old friends, whom she at least loves and values?"

Ernest rose hastily and silently from his seat. "I will be there almost as soon as yourself," exclaimed he; and indeed the countess had scarcely resumed her place at the upper end of the room, before she saw her son enter, and noted with delight, hidden under an air of proud humility, his graceful and high-born bearing. "He is odd, reserved, and studious," thought she; "but I shall make something of him yet."

But one eye, and one ear, was yet quicker than her own. Pauline was the first to see her cousin enter. She hastily turned aside, and began to be very much interested in some Bengal roses that stood beside; but her sigh was as soft, and almost as low, as their own, and her blush was still richer and deeper. Ernest came up and asked her to dance. Her eyes were downcast, and he thought she took his arm coldly; but more than one bystander remarked how different was the animation with which the young Baroness von Lindorf waltzed with her cousin, to that with which she had danced with the handsome Prince Louis.

At length the ball ended, as all balls do—having given some delight, more discontent, and also several colds; but it had answered the Countess's purpose. All Vienna talked of the approaching marriage of the beautiful heiress with Count von Hermanstadt. Many of her young friends ventured on a little gentle raillery. Pauline blushed, smiled, sighed, and denied the charge, but was believed by none. The time soon came for her return to the castle of Lindorf; but little of her life had been passed there. She had left it, when quite a child, for the convent, and of late she had spent much time with her aunt. Her father, a silent and reserved man, but doatingly fond of his child, came often to see her; and though Pauline could recollect nothing of the affectionate confidence which so often exists between father and daughter when left alone in the world, yet she was full of gratitude and tenderness. With the quick instinct of a loving heart, she saw that she was the Baron's first and only object—that her happiness, and even her girlish pleasures, were his constant care. There was something in his unbroken sadness, his habits of seclusion, and his gloomy deportment, that excited her youthful imagination, and gave a depth of anxious devotion to her filial attachment.

The paramount desire of the Baron appeared to be, that she should not find her home dull on returning to it. At his request the Countess von Hermanstadt had collected together a gay young party, and the old castle was for some weeks to be a scene of perpetual festival. Pauline went thither accompanied by her aunt and cousin. She at least found the journey delightful. Ernest, taken away from his books, animated by the fresh air and the rapid travelling, undisturbed by the presence of strangers, and anxious to please, now that he had no fear of either ridicule or coldness, was in high spirits. He drew their attention to every spot haunted by an association, and told its history as those tell who are steeped to the lip in poetry—rich in imagery, abounding in anecdote, he flung around all of which he spoke his own warm and fanciful feeling. Pauline fixed upon him her large blue eyes, where tenderness struggled with delight; while in the interest excited by his various details, she forgot the sweet and inward consciousness that would have fixed her eyes on the ground, or anywhere rather than on her cousin's face. The Countess was delighted to see everything going on so prosperously, and already began to plan wedding fêtes.

Night had fallen ere they approached the castle, the first view of which was singularly striking. The party had gradually sunk into silence, the road for miles had wound through a dense forest, with no other light than that flung over the road by the lamps of the carriage, and the torches which the out-riders carried before them, forming strange and fantastic outlines. The red light played over the drooping boughs of the forest trees; the flickering rays only illumined the outside, and all beyond was impenetrable obscurity: from the depths of that thick darkness came forth wild sighs and sounds; the mournful murmur of the pine leaves, the creaking of the branches as they swayed heavily in the wind; these, mingled with the hoarse cry of the night-birds. Sometimes disturbed from his gloomy perch, the dusk wings of the owl flapped across the road, and his hooting disturbed the sad low music of the night; it was neither time nor place for gay converse: the whole party felt the subduing influence, and leant back in deep thought. Suddenly they cleared the wood, and the carriage paused for a moment that they might catch the first view of the castle of Lindorf; visible for miles around,—there it stood in the centre of a vast plain, on the summit of a high hill, with not a single rise to intercept, or a single object to distract the view. It rose in bold relief against the deep blue sky, with the large round moon shining directly behind it;—even at that distance you could mark the square towers and the indented battlements, while the mass of the building itself seemed immense. The sky, of that intense purple which marks a slight frost, was covered with floating clouds, and on the further edge, sheltered in their shadow, were scattered a few pale stars; but the broadway of heaven was flooded by moonlight; no longer shut out by the thick forest,—her rays silvered whatever they touched, and the long grass of the plain looked like undulating water, so thickly did the crisped dew lie upon it, and so clearly did the moonshine glitter through the frosted moisture. Ernest gazed upon the dark and distant castle with an emotion for which he could not himself have accounted; he remembered it not—and yet it seemed strangely familiar. The moonlight clothed it like a garment, and the old towers shone like silver; but even while they gazed, the brightness was departing.—One mass of vapour flowed in after another like the dark tide coming in upon the shore; a black ridge rose above the castle; it darkened—it widened—its edges grew luminous as they approached the moon: gradually half her disk was hidden by them. "Is it an omen?" asked Ernest of his own thoughts. Even as he asked the question, the black cloud swept over the moon, and entire darkness covered the whole scene. "Drive on," cried Ernest, impatiently; and the horses set off at full gallop, but even the exhilaration of rapid motion failed to drive away the weight that had fallen upon his heart. He could not divest himself of the idea that the castle was in some way connected with his destiny,—and that such destiny was ill-fated. When at length they arrived, and drove slowly up the steep ascent as the old gate creaked on its hinges to receive them, and they alighted in the hall of black carved oak, he felt a cold shudder come over him. Again he asked himself—"Is it an omen?" and the voice of his inward spirit answered "Yes!"

A fortnight passed away, and one fête succeeded to another. At first Pauline clung to her cousin's side,—she wandered with him in the antique gardens, and would leave the dancers to gaze with him from the terrace which overlooked the vast plain below. Gradually she gave more and more into the pleasures around her; and the mornings were devoted to her young companions, and the evening saw her the gayest, as well as the loveliest of the assembled circle. This was a relief to Ernest—it left him more at liberty to indulge his own solitary pursuits, and to feed on the visionary melancholy, which was half thought—and half feeling. He was wrong, however, in the conclusion that he drew from the change in his cousin; he merely supposed that she was attracted by the amusements so natural to her age; he knew not that even that fair young brow had already learnt the bitter task of dissembling. He knew not that often did that bright young head lay down in weariness and sorrow on a pillow wet with frequent tears. Love only rightly interprets love. Pauline saw that her cousin had only for her the calm and gentle tenderness of a brother;—they had been brought up together, and there was nothing in the pretty and playful child, that had grown up beside him, to excite his imagination. But she—she loved him with all that poetry which is only to be found in a woman's first affection; it is the early colour that the rose-bud opens to the south wind,—the warmth that morning breathes upon a cloud whose blush reddens, but returns not. Pure, shy, sensitive, tender, and unreal; it is the most ethereal, yet most lasting feeling life can know. The influence of a woman's first love is felt on her whole after-existence: never can she dream such dream again. For a woman there is no second-love—youth, hope, belief, are all given to her first attachment; if unrequited, the heart becomes its own Prometheus, creative, ideal, but with the vulture preying upon it for ever.—If deceived, the whole poetry of life is gone; the very essence of poetry is belief, and how can she, whose sweet eager credulity has once learnt the bitter truth—that its reliance was in vain, how can she ever believe again?

Pauline learnt to know Ernest's heart by her own, and she felt the difference. Night after night she left the ball-room in all the false flutter of that excitement whose fever destroys the heart which it animates. But once in her own room, the colour left her cheek, and the light, her eye; she flung herself down, with a burst of tears, long and painfully repressed, while she thought that Ernest had not entered the hall throughout the evening. He, in the meanwhile, saw her seemingly happy and amused—and gave more and more into his pursuits; he would spend days in the old forest adjoining, till the midnight stars shone through the darkling branches like the eyes of a spirit, awakening all that was most ethereal in his nature. Hours too were past on the winding and lovely river—lost in those vague but impassioned reveries which fade, and for ever, amid the sterner realities of life. The dreaming boyhood prepares for adventurous man; we first fancy, then feel, and, at last, act and think. He delighted too in rambling through the ancient castle—filled with the memory of other days: not a face in the picture gallery but he conjured up its history, and he loved to assign to each some one of the spacious chambers for the site of their adventures. Many of the rooms in the left wing were all but deserted,—and one afternoon, while wandering carelessly along, he found his way into a chamber that had apparently not been opened for years; he was struck with the beauty of some richly wrought oak panels. While leaning against one of them he chanced to touch a hidden spring; the panel flew open—and discovered a narrow flight of winding stairs. To kindle a phosphorous match, to light a small wax taper, was the work of a moment; and he began to descent the staircase:—childishly eager to discover something—he did not much care what, so long as it was a discovery. It wound to a much greater distance than he had supposed, and, at last, ended at a sort of low arch—the door of which was heavily barred inside. With great difficulty he succeeded in unfastening it; at last it yielded to his efforts, and he opened it. It opened inwards—and even then, though he perceived the open air, he could scarcely make his way through the matted ivy, and the thickly grown shrubs that extended beyond. The moment he arrived beyond their shade he found himself in a position of the castle grounds which he had never seen before; it was a lovely little garden of small extent, girdled in by lofty walls and tall trees—but a fairy land in miniature as far as it extended. The hues of autumn were now upon the boughs—but the evergreens shone with untiring verdure; and various late flowers appeared in that gorgeous colouring which belongs to the last season of earth's fertility. He wound through a narrow path of green and purple,—for the carefully trained grapes hung in arches overhead, with fruit as rich as those of the eastern garden discovered by Aladdin. Ernest was enchanted with his discovery, and hurried on, when his attention was caught by the sound of singing; it was a female voice of the most touching sweetness. The words were inarticulate, but the air, an old German melody, was exquisitely marked. Ernest followed whither the voice led—he paused amid some laurel trees, and a scene like a picture presented itself to his astonished gaze; it was a bright open grass plot—a very rendezvous for every stray sunbeam,—and in the middle glittered and danced a little fountain which threw up its silvery jets in the air, and then fell over large shells, stones, and rugged pieces of granite, which formed a sort of basin; a number of creeping plants were around it, and one or two lilies grew as if carved in ivory. Seated on one of the huge stones scattered around—singing a low sweet air, or rather humming it, for the words were inaudible, was a female figure. Ernest could see only a very pretty back—and exquisitely shaped head bending forward, and a profusion of black hair hanging down in plaits—the ends somewhat fancifully fastened with a scarlet flower.

Ernest felt that he was an intruder, but he did—as all other young men would have done—remain rooted to the spot. He knew the melody that she was singing to the music of the splashing fountain; he had not heard it for years, but now it came freshly back to his memory haunted with a thousand vague fancies: suddenly the low sweet singing ceased; the maiden rose hastily from her seat, and, turning round, showed the exact likeness of his favourite picture—the Beatrice Cenci. There was not the peculiar head-gear,—for the hair was simply parted back; but everything else was exact in resemblance. There was the same low white forehead, the same black arched eyebrow, the same Grecian outline of face, the same small and scornful lip. She looked towards him, and there were the same large, dark, and melancholy eyes. Surprise made Ernest both speechless and motionless—not so the lovely stranger; she bounded towards him with something between the spring of the startled fawn, and the confidence of an eager child.

"I knew someone would come at last to free me from my weary captivity," exclaimed she, in one of those thrilling voices which have a magic beyond even their music; "you are not a prisoner too?" asked she, seeing the bewildered expression of Ernest's countenance.

"A prisoner! No," said he, too much astonished to know what he was saying, and taking one of the small and delicate hands which were extended so imploringly towards him.

"You will save me—help me, will you not?" asked the girl; "they have kept me here many years, and I long to go into the beautiful world that lies beyond these high walls. I sometimes wish I were a bird, and then I would spread my wings on the free air, and fly away, and be so happy. But you will take me with you, will you not?" whispered she, looking up in his face with the sweet and impatient look of a pleading child. "You look very kind—I may trust you, may I not?"

"With my life I will answer to that trust," cried young Hermanstadt; "but who are you,—who keeps you here?"

"My uncle, the Baron von Lindorf," muttered she, in a low frightened voice. "They tell me that there is a castle, and vassals, and gold, that should be mine, and that is why he keeps me here. He is very cruel!"

"Good God!" cried Ernest, "come this moment with me—and in his usurped place—before his own guests—I will force him to do you right."

"No, no," replied the captive, her lip whitening, and the pupils of her large eyes dilating with sudden terror. "No, let us fly,—you do not know how cruel he is, and how strong. Let us only get beyond these high walls. How did you get in?"

"I found by chance a long, concealed passage."

"And you can come again? Ah! now I shall not mind being a prisoner. You will come and talk to me—and not tell me to be quiet, like old Clotilde, or frown upon me like Heinrich?"

"You shall not stay here—come with me this moment. I will protect you from them all!"

"No," replied the captive, "not now; you do not know my uncle's power—he would kill us both; we must escape without his knowing it. Do you think you can manage it in a few days?"

"Certainly! but the sooner the better."

"What is your name?" interrupted the prisoner.

"Ernest von Hermanstadt."

"They call me Minna. I used to have another name, but it is so long ago that I have forgotten it; I have grown so much since I was here. I could not reach those flowers when I came here first;—my pretty flowers, and my singing fountain—I shall be sorry to leave you! You never scold Minna; but it is a brave world yonder—you will take me into it, Ernest?" asked she; and again those sweet eyes were raised beseechingly to his.

"Come with me now—I will pledge my life for your safety!"

"No, come to-morrow—can you—without being seen? To-morrow morning, when those clouds are reddening, and the waters of the fountain are rosy with their shadows? I always come here then, I love the fresh air of the morning."

At this moment a shrill voice in the distance was heard calling—"Minna, Minna." Ernest would have pressed forward, when the maiden caught his arm, trembling from head to foot. "Go, go," whispered she, then, clasping her little hands with an air of passionate entreaty, she added:—"I expect you to-morrow at sunrise;" and before he could answer, she had darted away. Once she looked back, but it was to wave her hand in token that he should depart. Ernest lingered for a moment, and then hurried back to the hidden passage; he carefully effaced all traces of his progress—and drew the ivy after him when he entered the arched door, that he barred; and then hurriedly sought his own chamber, which he left no more that night. This was an act of too frequent occurrence, on his part, to excite the least surprise; and the supposed student was left undisturbed,—for, for him there was as little study as rest. That sweet face floated before his eyes, that low melodious voice haunted his ear—and the name of Minna lingered upon his lip. "Now," thought he, "I understand the cause of my uncle's gloom and abstraction; no marvel that he has no heart for gaiety with such a crime pressing upon it. I faintly remember hearing that his brother had fallen in some campaign that they fought together;—doubtless, with his last breath he commended his orphan girl to one bound by blood to protect her. How has that dying trust been violated; how has that child been oppressed! Made a prisoner—debarred all the social enjoyments of her age—deprived of rank and birthright, immured in solitude and ignorance. Great God! can such cruelty exist among the creatures thou has made? but retribution, sooner or later, overtakes the guilty. Poor Pauline! how will her gentle and affectionate nature be grieved to hear this thing of the father she idolises; it must be kept from her. Wealth, what a subtle tempter thou art! Even my uncle—the man I deemed so noble, so generous, so full of high feeling, and knightly qualities; even he has for thy sake played traitor to the dead, and broken every sacred tie of duty and of affection! I will think no more of it." This resolve was easily executed; for the image of Minna excluded every other thought. Her beauty, her grace, her childishness had captivated Ernest's imagination; fate, too, had set her stamp upon the fiery passion to which he utterly abandoned himself. "How strangely," murmured he to himself, as, thrown in the deep window-seat, he gazed out upon the silent night—"are the links knitted together, which time unravels! The picture my boyhood discovered, and which so haunted my youth, has it not now fulfilled its mission? The chance likeness has led to the predestined result. I feel it,—Minna has been predestined to be my bride. Fate, in filling my heart with her face, from the earliest years kept it free from all those passing fancies which would have detracted from the intense devotion of my present love. How wonderfully have we met! Minna—sweet Minna, life owes you much happiness; will it not be my delicious task to pay the debt?"

The night passed in one long, but happy reverie; and the light sleep into which Ernest fell at last was soon broken by the anxiety, which visited even his dreams, to catch the first crimson break of morning. He started from his bed—and the dark clouds in the east were beginning to redden; he hurried to the deserted suite of rooms—down the winding staircase, and in a few moments found himself again in the little garden. Cautiously he entered the vine-covered alley, and paused for a moment amid the thick shelter of the laurels; with a glance he drank in the beauty of the scene; the feeling of the painter and the poet—and Ernest had the imagination of both overpowered, during an instant, the feeling of the lover. Huge bodies of vapour—a storm in each—were hurrying over a sky, dashed alike with the hues of the tempest and the morning; some of the vapours were of inky blackness, others spread like a scroll of royal purple; some undulated with the light struggling through, others were of transparent whiteness; but those upon the east were of a deep crimson—and the round, red sun had just mounted above an enormous old cedar. Red hues were cast upon everything; even the lilies blushed, and the waters of the little fountain were like melted rubies: on the same stone which she had occupied the previous day sat Minna, but her head was now turned towards the spot where she had last seen Ernest. A movement amid the boughs caught her quick ear; she started from her seat upon the granite, and Ernest was at her feet. Shy, silent, with her long eyelashes drooping upon her flushed cheek; there was a sweet consciousness about her—even more fascinating than her yesterday's childish confidence. Ernest led her to her place, and knelt beside her; he had no words but those of love; he had a thousand plans for the future ready on his tongue; he could only speak of the present. "Yes, Minna; may I not call you so, though I am jealous of the very air bearing away the music of that name? I have loved you for years: not a feature in that beautiful face but has been long graven in my soul. I will show you your picture, sweet one, when you come home with me. Will you come to my home?"

And the maiden smiled and said, "I shall be so happy."

But the words of lovers are a language apart; their melody is a fairy song departing with the one haunted hour; to repeat it is to make it commonplace—cold, yet we can all remember it. Enough, that everything was planned for flight. The following morning they were to meet again; and Minna was only to return to the castle of Lindorf as the bride of Ernest von Hermanstadt. None there could question his right to protect her. The clouds gathered overhead; a vast vapour like a shroud, but black as night, came sweeping over the sky; a fierce wind shook the branches of the mighty cedar, and the slighter shrubs were bowed to the very earth; a hollow sound came from among the boughs, and a few large drops of rain disturbed the fountain, whose waters were dark as if the sunshine had never rested there.

"You must go, sweet one; this is no weather for that slight form. To-morrow, at sunset—"

"Why cannot I give you this?" exclaimed Minna, holding up one of the tresses with its scarlet flower.

"You must," cried Ernest, kissing the plait of the black hair, which was soft and glossy as the neck of the raven.

"I have nothing," said she, sadly, "that I can cut it with."

Ernest took from his pocket a little Turkish dagger—and with that Minna severed the glossy tress.

"I must go now," said she, "they will seek me if I stay out in the rain."

Ernest pressed her tenderly to his heart, and they parted. He caught the last wave of the flowers in her hair—the last sound of her fairy foot, and turned mournfully away. All that day he was occupied in preparations for his departure; he rode over to the castle of Krainberg which belonged to a fellow student, whom he found on the point of departure. The young Baron, delighted with the romance, of which however he understood little more than that his grave and quiet friend was actually engaged in an elopement—agreed to remain to witness the marriage. He was also to have his chapel prepared, a priest in readiness, and then to leave his castle as a temporary residence for the bride and bridegroom. His mother had left Lindorf—or he would have trusted his secret with her and entreated her countenance. In his own mind, Ernest was not sorry that her absence rendered this impossible; he liked the excitement, the strangeness, the adventure of his present plan, and his mother's calm and worldly temper would have interposed a thousand delays, and have arranged everything in the most proper and common-place manner.

He was early at their rendezvous, the fountain, but early as he was, Minna was there before him; she approached him in a hurried and agitated manner, her slight frame trembling with emotion, her large eyes glancing from side to side like those of the frightened deer—and he could feel every pulse beating in the little feverish hand, which he kissed.

"Let us go at once," whispered she, "they will soon come to seek me." Ernest needed no urging to speed; he led, or almost carried her, down the vine alley, and they reached the dark portal without molestation. Minna drew back, terrified at the gloomy passage—but Ernest's caresses reassured her, and she ran up the winding stairs; in a short time they reached the little chamber, which was his study, and that gained, they were in comparative safety. Here they waited a short time, partly to give the lovely fugitive time to compose herself—partly, that it might be dusk before they attempted to leave the castle: that, however, was matter of no difficulty. A staircase led direct from Ernest's chamber to the garden—and he had the key of a small wicket which led to the woods around; once there, and escape was certain. Minna sat down in the old oak chair, which was Ernest's usual place. With what delight did he contemplate her charming figure bending over the table, and examining his favourite volumes with a curiosity which even fear and timidity could not quite dispel! what a delicious augury did the enthusiastic young student draw from her apparent interest! How many happy hours would they pass together over those very volumes! but there was little time even for the most delightful anticipations of the future. The dinner hour of the castle had now arrived—and every creature in it was busily engaged. Now then was the time to leave it. Carefully wrapping up his precious charge in his cloak, he led her to the little gate, where his servant was in waiting. Placing her before him, he sprung up on his horse, a strong and stately black steed, and a few moments more saw them galloping rapidly along the road that led to Arnheim castle. They needed to make all possible haste, for the storm, which had been gathering all day, now threatened to burst over their heads:—their way lay through a thick wood—and the elements had already commenced their strife. The creaking of the huge pine branches, mixed with the hurried sweeping of the leaves, of which a dry shower every now and them whirled from the earth— from the gathered heaps of autumn, or came down in hundreds from overhead. The birds, disturbed from their usual rest, flew around, beating the air with their troubled wings, and uttering shrill cries; the thunder rolled along in the distance, and a few large drops of rain fell heavily upon the ground; there was an unnatural heat in the air, and gleams of phosphoric light streamed along the burthened sky. But

Ernest heeded not the storm; he only feared for the sweet burthen that rested so trustingly in his arms—he only drank the perfumed breath of the warm lips so near his own; he only felt the beating of the heart, now and henceforth to be pillowed on his own; he only heard the low murmur of a voice which now and then whispered his name—as if that name were to her all of love and safety. He spurred his horse to its utmost speed; the sparks flew from its hoof. He cut his way through the fresh wind, and felt as if the excitement of the impassioned moment were cheaply purchased, though his life were its ransom. They reached the castle of Krainberg before the storm burst forth in all its fury. The master was in waiting to receive them, and Ernest felt all a lover's pride as he marked the astonishment and admiration with which Von Krainberg gazed on the beautiful stranger. They led her at once to the chapel; Ernest grudged himself the pleasure of even seeing her till he had a right to gaze upon her—till every look was at once homage and protection; he was impatient, in her strange and isolated situation, to call her his own—his wife. A close, damp air struck upon them as they entered the chapel; it had long been out of use, and the hastily lighted tapers burnt dim in the sepulchral atmosphere. The mouldering banners were stirred by the high wind, and the breathing was oppressed by the dust; many tombs were around, and the white effigies seemed like reluctant witnesses glaring upon the hopes of humanity, with cold and stony eyes. A monk, bowed with extreme age, pale, emaciated, and his white head tremulous with palsy, stood beside the altar—and his long, thin fingers trembled beneath the weight of the sacred volume. He began the ceremony, and his low, tremulous voice could scarcely be heard through the moaning of the wind amid the tombs. The ground beneath their feet was hollow, and sent forth a hollow echo;—the graves below had once been filled with the dead, and now only a little dust remained in their vacant places: they had perished as it were a second time. There was a mournful contrast between the place of the bridal and the bride; there she stood in that radiant loveliness, which is heaven's rarest gift to earth. Her dress was of the simplest white, gathered at the waist by a belt of her own embroidery—ornament she had none. The daughter of the noble house of Von Lindorf wedded the heir of the as noble house of Von Hermanstadt dressed as simply as a peasant. Her black hair hung down in its long plaits, like serpents—the scarlet flower at each end; a bright colour flushed her cheek, and her eyes seemed filled with light.

The aged priest closed the holy book, and Ernest turned to salute his bride; but even he started back at the sudden clap of thunder that pealed through the chapel. The building shook beneath the crash, and a flood of lightning poured in at the windows, casting a death-like light on the stony faces of the white figures on the monuments:—it was but for a moment—and Ernest caught his trembling bride to his heart. She was pale with terror, for now the storm rushed forth in all its fury, and a sudden gust of wind and rain dashed against the painted window at the end of the chapel. The repeated flashes threw a strange radiance around, and strange noises mingled together.

"It is an awful night," said the young baron of Krainberg, as he led the way to the hall, which, as they entered, was lit up with one livid blaze. Ernest supported the almost insensible form of his bride; he murmured a few caressing words—but even love, in all its strength, felt powerless before the war of the immortal elements.

The next morning but few traces of the tempest remained; the river that wound through the valley was somewhat swollen, and a few giant pines dashed down to earth would never again cast their long shadows before them on a summer morning; but the sky was soft, clear, and blue, and a few white clouds wandered past, light as down. The leaves glittered with the lingering rain-drops, and a fresh, sweet smell came from the herbage of the valley. Ernest was seated in a little breakfast parlour, looking to a terrace that commanded the country; he was seated at the feet of his bride, whose small fingers were entwined in his black hair. What a world of poetry seemed in the depths of her large, shining eyes, which looked upon him so tenderly—so timidly; their dream, for it was a dream-like happiness, was broken in upon by the entrance of Ernest's servant, who asked to speak to his master. There was something in the man's manner which commanded instant attention, and Von Hermanstadt followed him out of the room.

"Sir," exclaimed the man, "here is your letter to the Baron—he died suddenly last night. The lady Pauline is in a dreadful state, and the steward entreated that you would go up there at once."

Ernest felt that this was case which admitted of no delay. Saying a few hasty words about important business to Minna, reserving the death till he could have time to tell it soothingly, he flung himself upon his horse, and galloped to Lindorf. Though grave and solitary, both in manners and habits, the Baron had been much beloved by his domestics, and the voice of weeping was heard on every side. Ernest hurried to his uncle's chamber; there the daylight was excluded, and the ray of the yellow tapers fell dimly upon the green velvet bed where lay the last Baron of Lindorf. In him ended that noble house; with his arms folded, so as to press the ebon crucifix to his bosom—his head supported by a damask cushion, lay the Baron. Ernest paused for a moment, awe-struck by the calm beauty which reigned in the face of the dead; the features were stately and calm, the brow had lost the care-worn look it wore in life, and peace breathed from every lineament of the sweet and hushed countenance. "Can the dead," thought Ernest, "struck down with an unrepented crime—can the oppressor of the orphan look thus?"

He had not time for further reflection, for a convulsive motion on the other side of the bed showed him Pauline crouched in a heap at the feet of the corpse—her face buried in the silken counterpane. Her bright hair was knit up with pearls, and she still wore the robe of the previous evening; how terrible seemed its gay colours now!

"We have not been able," whispered an old grey-headed servant, "to get her to speak or to move."

Ernest's heart melted with the tenderest pity. He took the passive hand, and covered it with tears and kisses. "Pauline, dearest, look up," said he, passing his arm round her, so as to raise her head. What his words could not effect, the movement did; she was roused from her stupor, and giving one wild glance at the corpse, she leant her head on her cousin's shoulder, and burst into a passion of tears. Soothing her with the tenderest words, he carried her to her chamber. "At least," said he to himself, as he left her, "the memory of her father shall be sacred."

The old steward met him, and said—"There is a letter for you which my master was writing at the time of his death. I know many circumstances which it is now of the last importance that you should know too. For God's sake, Sir, go and read the letter, and I will be within call."

The old man led the way to his master's room. He looked round it piteously for a moment, and then hurried away, hiding his face in his hands. Ernest had never been in the room before; and yet how full it seemed of the living presence of him who was no more! There was his cloak flung on a chair;—there lay open books of which he and Ernest had recently been talking. There, too, was a flask of medicine—alas! how unavailing!—and a goblet of water, half drank. But one object more than all riveted Ernest's attention;—there was the picture of Beatrice Cenci. It was a portrait as large as life: his own seemed to have been a copy of it. How well he knew that striking and lovely face! He knew not why, but he gazed upon it with a sudden terror; the large black eyes seemed to fix so mournfully upon his own. He turned away, and saw the letter on the table, addressed to himself. He seated himself, and began to read the contents; though the tears swam in his eyes as he saw the handwriting of an uncle who, whatever his faults, had always been kind, very kind, to himself. It ran thus:—

"My beloved Ernest,—For dear to me as a child of my own is the boy who has grown up at my side. I have long been desirous of communicating to you the contents of the following pages, but I have found it too painful to speak—I find that I must write. My confidence will not be misplaced, for I have noted in you a judgment beyond your years, and a delicacy which will estimate the trust reposed in you. My health is declining rapidly, and I would fain secure protection for my darling Pauline, and another as dear and more unfortunate. I have rejoiced to see that my sister's plan for a marriage between you and my daughter is not likely to take place. You do not love your cousin—you prefer the solitary study and the lonely ramble—so would not a lover. She, too, is amused in your absence. I hear her step and song among her companions, and you are not with them. It is for the best—you will be a safe and affectionate friend. I hope she will never marry.

"Alas!—On me and mine has rested a fearful curse! I married one whose beauty let the picture now opposite to me attest, and her heart was even lovelier than her face. An Italian artist painted her as Beatrice Cenci: he said that the costume suited her so well. I have since thought it an omen that we should have chosen the semblance of one so ill-fated. For years we were most happy, but at last an unaccountable depression seized upon my wife. She became wayward and irritable. This led to the quarrel between your mother and ourselves. She knew not the fatal cause. After the birth of her third and last child, her malady took a darker turn. Ernest, it was melancholy madness, and incurable! In a paroxysm of despondency, she murdered the infant in her arms, and died a few hours afterwards in a state of raving insanity!

"I will not dwell on my after-years of misery. I was roused by fear of the headstrong and violent temper of my eldest girl, Minna—I saw in it the seeds of her mother's malady. My terror was too well founded. She was found one evening attempting to strangle her little sleeping sister, who was then six years old—Minna being just fourteen. A brain fever followed, and a report was spread of her death. Why should our family calamity be made the topic of idle curiosity? But, in reality, she has resided in this castle—her state requiring constant and often strict restraint. I have been scarcely ever absent from the castle; but, alas! my tenderness has answered but in part. With a caprice incidental to persons in her dreadful situation, she has taken an extreme dislike to me, and fancies that I am her uncle, and imprison her to detain the vast possessions of which she fancies herself the heiress."

The fatal paper dropped from Ernest's hand. He remained pale, breathless, the dew starting, and the veins swelled of his forehead. "God of heaven, have mercy on me!—What have I done?" Again he caught up the letter, and, with a desperate effort, read to the close.

"My faithful Heinrich and his sister Clotilde are the only depositories of this secret. While I live, I shall devote myself to the care of my ill-starred Minna, who is the very image of her mother. When I die—and the shadow of death even now rests upon my way—I commend her to her God and to you. You will be to her and to Pauline as a brother. I know I can rely upon you."

"Married to a maniac—a hopeless maniac!—What will my mother say?"—exclaimed Ernest, as he paced the room. The image of his beautiful bride rose before him; he felt as if his tenderness and his devotion must avail; he would watch her every look—anticipate her very thoughts. He started—it was the steward who came into the room.

"I see," said the old man, "that you have read my master's letter. Alas! I have dreadful news to tell. The Baroness Minna has evaded all our precautions. She has escaped, I know not whither. I only trust that it is alone."

"Heinrich," said Ernest, solemnly, "I speak to you as the trusted and valued friend of my beloved uncle. Minna is with me. I married her last night—deceived, alas! by a narrative which I ought never to have credited. I at least ought to have known my uncle too well to believe that he could be guilty of fraud or oppression. The rest of my life will be too little to atone for that moment's doubt. Old man, hear me swear to devote myself to his children!"

"God bless you!" sobbed the old man, as he clasped the hand which Ernest extended towards him.

Months passed away in unceasing watchfulness on the part of Ernest. With trembling hope he began to rely on Minna's complete recovery. Wild she was at times, and her fondness for him had a strange character of fierceness; but his influence over her was unbounded, and her passion for music was a constant resource. By Heinrich's advice they left the castle, that no painful train of thought might be awakened; and they resided in a light, cheerful villa, amid the suburbs of Vienna. Her husband found all the plans of mutual study in which the young student lover had so delighted, were in vain. It was impossible to fix her attention long on anything. Companionship there was none between them, and the call on his attention was unceasing; but his affection became even deeper for its very fear, and it was hallowed by the feeling of how sacred it was as a duty. Gradually as he became more and more satisfied about Minna, he grew more anxious for Pauline. He saw her drooping day by day; her spirits became unequal, and her eyes were rarely without tears. Too late he discovered how she loved him. Her bodily weakness seemed to render her less capable of repressing her feelings. Her eye followed him, go where he would; she hung upon his least word, and she shrunk away from her sister. The proposed visit to his mother brought on such a passion of tears, that he had not the heart to insist upon it—especially when he looked upon her pale, sunken cheek, and watched her slow dispirited step. Once or twice he saw Minna watching her with a wild, strange glance in her large, black eyes, as if there was an intensive feeling of jealousy.

It was now the first week in June, and the weather was unusually hot; and there was thunder in the air, which added to the oppression. The moon, too, was at its full; and Minna, always restless at that time, was now unusually so. At last, towards evening, she sank on the window-seat in a deep slumber. Pauline was walking on the terrace below; and Ernest, who saw that she was scarcely equal to the fatigue, went down to give her his assistance. She took his arm, and they walked up and down together. At last she leant over the balustrade, and her eyes filled with tears as she watched the moonlight turning the flowers to silver.

"I wish," said she, "I were a flower—happy in the sunshine—happy in the soft night air. No beating heart within, to make me wretched." And she dropped her head on his arm, and wept.

Before Ernest has time to utter even a few soothing words, a bright blade glittered in the moonlight, and Pauline sunk with a faint scream on the pavement—Minna had stabbed her sister to the heart! There she stood: her cheek flushed with the deepest crimson, and her eyes flashing the wild light of insanity— waving the weapon she had so fatally used. It was the little Indian dagger Ernest had lent her to sever the song tress of hair. She had concealed it till this moment.

"Yes," cried she, "I have killed her at last. They thought I did not know her, but I did. She took away my father's heart from me, and would have taken away my husband's; but I have killed her at last."

By this time the servants came rushing from all parts. At their approach, Minna seemed seized with some vague fear, and attempted to fly. Ernest had just time to pass his arms around her, thought she struggled violently. They raised Pauline, but the last spark of life had fled—the pale and lovely features were set in death!

Minna lived on for years—her insanity taking, every succeeding year, a darker colour. Ernest never left her side. Fierce of sullen, violent or desponding, he watched her through every mood. She wore herself away to a shadow, till it was a marvel how that frail form endured. For months before her death, she was almost ungovernable, and did not know him the least. She scarcely ever slept, but one night slumber overpowered her. The sun was shining brightly into the chamber, and its light fell upon the whitened hair and careworn features of her husband, who had been watching by her for hours. A sweet and meek expression was in her eyes when she awoke.

"Ernest, dearest Ernest," said she, in a soft, low whisper. She raised her head from the pillow, and, like a child, put up her mouth to kiss him. She sank back: her last breath had passed in that kiss!

He laid her in the same tomb with her father and sister; and the next day, the noble, the wealthy, and still handsome Count von Hermanstadt entered the order of St. Francis.

www.ingramcontent.com/pod-product-compliance
Lightning Source LLC
Chambersburg PA
CBHW072039170626
46811CB00008B/3110